HANDCUFFING THE ALIEN

BEASTLY ALIEN BOSS, BOOK 6

AVA ROSS

HANDCUFFING THE ALIEN

Beastly Alien Boss Series, Book 6

Copyright © 2023 Ava Ross

All rights reserved.

No part of this book may be reproduced in any form or by any electronic or mechanical means, including information storage and retrieval systems, without written permission from the author, except for the use of brief quotations with prior approval. Names, characters, events, and incidents are a product of the author's imagination. Any resemblance to an actual person, living or dead is entirely coincidental.

Cover art by Natasha Snow Designs

Editing: JA Wren

Proofreading by Owl Eyes Proofs & Edits & Sydnee Walsh

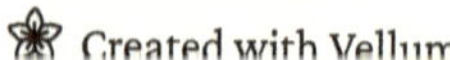 Created with Vellum

A note to the reader.

If you found this book outside of Amazon,
it's likely a stolen/pirated copy.
Authors make nothing when books are pirated.
If authors are not paid for their work,
they can't afford to keep writing.

SERIES BY AVA

Mail-Order Brides of Crakair

Brides of Driegon

Fated Mates of the Ferlaern Warriors

Fated Mates of the Xilan Warriors

Holiday with a Cu'zod Warrior

Galaxy Games

Alien Warrior Abandoned/
Shattered Galaxies

Beastly Alien Boss

Bride of the Fae

A Sci-Fi Holiday Tail

Monsterville, USA
(Includes Monster Between the Sheets &
Sweet Monster Treats)

Monster on Board
(co-written with Alana Khan)

You can find my books on Amazon.

HANDCUFFING THE ALIEN

My alien hero not only wants to rescue me, but he also wants to claim me too.

Wrongfully convicted of murder and sentenced to hard labor on an alien prison planet, I think my life is over. Until my rescue comes in the form of my older brother's best friend, Shaede—a blue-skinned alien who broke my heart years ago. But he gets caught too, and before you know it, we're handcuffed together and locked in a cell with only one bunk.

Shaede is determined to save us, no matter the cost. And in the meantime, he plans to convince me that he made a big mistake turning me down. He wants to claim me as his mate . . .

Handcuffing the Alien is Book 6 in the Beastly Alien Boss Series. Each book is loosely connected and features an

Earth woman hired for an off-world job who meets a gruff alien who can't resist falling for his fated mate.

CHAPTER ONE
CHARLIE

"See the galaxies," the Interstellar Employment Agency employee told me. "Enjoy new foods and meet exciting alien people!"

I doubted the guy at the Agency had a Vassar jail in mind when he said that. Neither did I.

I'd just been laid off by Interstellar Interpol, so when the opportunity to travel to the Plushier Space Station to provide security for a Match-Mating Soiree came up, I jumped. It wasn't my usual kind of assignment. Who expected to make a drug bust during a matchmaking event?

But a recent split with a decent guy who just wasn't right gave me the extra push I needed to take the job. He was one in a long string of guys who also weren't "right" thanks to my teenage crush, Shaede, who stomped all over my heart. He made me see any guy I'd met since then was not quite enough.

There was nothing wrong with a woman pining for an alien hottie who turned her down, correct?

Okay, so it *had* been six years, but the pinch still thrived in my heart.

If the alien lizard mafia, the Vessars, hadn't tried to infiltrate the Soiree, and I hadn't knocked a bunch of them out, they wouldn't have kidnapped me and sent me to their prison planet.

It was funny how one simple move could take a woman's life in a completely different direction.

And now, here I was, sneaking around the prison while everyone else slept.

As I stood in the hall between the long row of prison cells, I hitched my wig lower on my forehead. A quick swipe of my finger told me my auburn tresses weren't peeking out from beneath the fake hair. A glance down told me my uniform looked like everyone else's and that my boobs remained bound beneath the snug cloth encircling my chest.

In case any of my fellow inmates were watching, I made sure my pace resembled that of a guy. I thanked all that was fated that the warden and my fellow inmates hadn't seen past the disguise I donned while locked inside the hold of the Vessar ship that brought me here. Everyone thought I was a teenage boy. It paid to keep a wig and binder on your person at all times.

Maybe my boss shouldn't have been so hasty in laying me off. Look at me, working for free on the case he'd quashed, stating we'd never figure out what the Vessars were up to on their prison planet.

Tonight, I'd completed another reconnaissance mission that went nowhere, so maybe my boss hadn't been that far off in his assumption this case was dead.

A niggling feeling in the middle of my spine—the area that still ached from when I jumped a hornburr on Quixan 5 and he fought back—told me something odd was going on here. If only I could figure it out. I'd snuck out of my cell to search the areas of the compound I could reach as often as I could during the lunar cycle I'd been incarcerated here, but I hadn't found much to build a case on.

My cell door gave way with a subtle creak when I pushed it open, making me freeze and peer around.

A soft cheep echoed behind me, and I jumped. Turning, I scooped Rosie up from the stone floor. I'd befriended the rodent-like creature within a dia of arriving here. She'd popped out from beneath my bunk and climbed onto my chest. I assumed she'd been tamed by whoever occupied the cell before me.

The whiskers on the tip of her long nose twitched, and her long tail coiled around my wrist, holding tight.

I stroked her fluffy pale blue fur and listened.

When no one called out, I slipped inside my cell and pulled the barred door shut. My heart stalled when the lock clicked into place, and I worried my lower lip with my teeth, wondering if I'd have time to discover the warden's plan before my guise was discovered.

With a grunt, I kicked off my boots and sank onto my hard bunk, lowering Rosie to my side. She coiled close to my warmth and sighed. I dragged the scratchy blanket over us and rubbed my face with my palms. There was nothing I could do but continue this mission.

When I disarmed the Vessars on the space station during the Match-Mating Soiree, I never thought they'd grab me. They'd tossed me into the hold of their ship, where I quickly donned my disguise. Other Vessars brought me to the prison planet, where they put me through a hasty trial where I wasn't given the chance to defend myself. A grainy vid showed me "assaulting" the Vessars, and that was all the "jury" of angry lizards needed.

I was sentenced to one yaro hard labor that would've been served on my back if they realized I was female.

Like all the other able-bodied inmates, they sent me to work in the mines.

If I were lucky, I'd continue to provide them with what they sought over everything else until I'd gathered enough information and could flee. I worried I wouldn't be able to keep them satisfied with my haul since they *really* loved what I retrieved from beneath the planet's surface.

After tossing and turning for a while, I gave up on sleeping and stared at the ceiling. Rosie's soft snores erupted from beside me, and I stroked her fur, grateful I had her as a friend.

The barred narrow window mounted in the stone wall on my left let in a slip of dawn. Guards would be here soon to escort me to my next day at work.

I tossed my holey blanket to the side and slid off the bunk, covering Rosie so she could keep sleeping. I crossed to the wall near the foot of my bed and made a careful mark in a stone slab. Thirty-one. Only three-hundred and thirty-four dias left in my sentence.

Yeah, I'd escape long before that.

I should crawl back onto my bunk and suck in the bit of heat I'd left behind, but all I could think of was what I would attempt soon. I'd searched most of the main prison building and a few of the nearby structures, and it was time to check out the rest of the compound. Unfortunately, I'd be in full view of the guards at the top of the wall when I crossed the open areas between here and the buildings.

Pacing the tiny space, my bare feet silent on the stone floor, I ticked everything on my list for the thousandth time. Once I'd discovered the prison's secrets, I'd have to flee.

Food and water were hidden away.

Both had come at some expense to my body, but it should be enough to get me across the wasteland surrounding the prison. Once I'd reached the other side, I'd find a way off this forsaken planet. Then, I'd beat down my former boss's door and show him the evidence I'd worked hard to obtain—assuming I could obtain it.

I'd send reinforcements to free my fellow prisoners.

Would the credits I'd gained in trades with the guards be enough to buy my passage off tho planet? Maybe I should trade for a few more.

I'd already hidden a sack of clothing with everything else.

What else did I need? I'd spent every waking moment

going through my final escape plan until it felt seamless, but there were so many unknown variables that might trip me up.

What if I—

Footsteps whispered in the hall.

I fled to my bunk. Only the shift of the blanket betrayed me as I tucked myself in beside Rosie.

I punctured the dawn with a low groan and muttered something incomprehensible to add to the impression I was having a nightmare. There was nothing new about that. My dreams had been haunted by images of someone grabbing me while I mined and realizing there was a female hidden beneath my dirty clothing.

If the vein of brugeer I'd discovered ran out and I didn't find another, they might send me to a different mine to work. Then I'd have to start all over again, hiding food, water, and whatever else I'd need to escape across the wasteland.

Only the brugeer kept me safe. That and one of the inmates watching out for me. He said I reminded him of his little brother, which made me laugh inside.

Turning, I faced the door to my cell. It was still dark enough that whoever approached would think me asleep, even with my eyes slitted. A person could never be too careful, especially with lizard aliens.

The footsteps came closer, and the person paused outside my cell, watching me. When a series of low clicks rang out, I tensed.

"Charlie," a male voice whispered, his face hidden in shadows.

Tall. Bulky. Maybe bluish skin. He wasn't one of my fellow lizard prisoners or a guard.

Tension spiked through me. I didn't like change.

"Charlie? Shit, are you dead?" Desperation came through in the guy's voice.

My breath caught.

No, no, no.

It couldn't be *him*.

It had been six yaros. I had to be mistaken.

Shaede Dil'in Chorkain couldn't be standing on the other side of my cell door.

"Go away," I snarled.

Really lame there, Charlie, the voice on my right shoulder—my conscience—said. *Really lame.*

She's wise, the voice on my left shoulder—my snarky side—said.

When a girl was locked up for over a month, she had to talk to someone other than a fluffy blue rodent.

"Is that how you treat your rescuer?" The cocky self-confidence in the guy's voice had been branded into my skin yaros ago.

Back then, I'd been a newly minted eighteen-year-old to his twenty-four, but me finally being legal hadn't made me appealing enough for a hot-shot interstellar agent like him.

"I said go away." I had to be dreaming. No, it was a true nightmare.

"Get out of bed, Charlie. I'm getting your ass out of here."

The last time I'd heard that cultured voice, the same

snideness had come through in his oh-so-polite but just as devastating rejection.

Light grew in the cell, revealing he hadn't changed a bit since I last saw him.

I skimmed my gaze down his tall, broad body, taking in the new scar on his silvery blue face. I hoped to find flaws that would make it easier to forget how I threw myself at him only for him to tell me I was too young. Too innocent. Too unappealing. He hadn't outright named the last, but it had come through loud and clear in his voice.

He shoved back a strand of his white hair, revealing piercing blue eyes that had caught and held me the minue I met him—when my older brother brought home the best friend he'd met at interstellar cop training.

An alien as well, Matis wasn't my blood brother, but he took me under his wing when I was five to his fourteen. He'd protected me from the other kids at the orphanage, and we'd been close ever since.

When I met Shaede, I was seventeen and still living at the orphanage. Back then, my eyes were full of stars after the tales Matis shared about spaceships and danger. I'd seen Shaede as a hero just like the brother I looked up to. A warrior. Someone I could fall in love with.

He'd generated a galaxy of dreams for my poor little heart. Until he stomped those dreams into the ground.

"At least you're not dead." He cleared his throat and kept his tone low. Wise on his part. The guys around me slept lightly. One never knew what might creep up on you while you slumbered. "I'm here to rescue you."

"I'm not ready to leave yet," I hissed. Despite wanting to turn my back on him and pretend he didn't exist, I flicked back the blanket and sat on the edge of my bunk.

Rosie hopped onto the floor and scurried beneath, hiding.

Shaede lounged against the bars. "That makes absolutely no sense. Put your boots on and step in line, soldier."

"You're not my boss."

"Same thing."

"Not even close."

"*I'm* in charge of this mission."

"Not as far as *I'm* concerned."

"I'm not going to argue with you about it. Matis sent word you were here, and I've come to rescue you."

"Where is Matis?" I'd expected my brother to find a way to free me, not asked Shaede to do it for him.

"He's . . . not available."

On a mission, then.

"That's why you've got me," Shaede added.

Interesting way of phrasing it. If only my silly heart didn't flop around at the thought of "having" Shaede.

"I don't need you." Want and need were two different things, and I could keep the first from snatching control and running away with my soul. I was no longer eighteen and innocent. As for unappealing, there wasn't much a woman could do about something like that, especially while wearing a black wig and chest binder.

Who the hell cared what Shaede thought about me? I

hated that the hard shell around my heart might still have a crack wide enough for him to creep back inside.

"When I'm ready to leave, I'll get out of here on my own," I said.

"You're locked in a cell." His cocky chuckle rang out.

"Don't laugh. And I'm not locked in."

"Not laughing. And you are."

It was his smirk that made me want to snarl, the same one he'd displayed six yaros ago when he shot me down. Fury blazed across my soul.

He gripped the bars, and I noted a pack slouched by his feet. "You want out or not?"

Even if I needed help, he'd be the last one I'd hand my fate to.

"You need to leave," I said, hopping off the bunk and stuffing my feet into my boots. "I'll be along eventually."

His gaze traveled down my frame in a way it hadn't six yaros ago.

Like one glance from Shaede could hit a switch no one else had discovered, my veins pulsed madly. I wore grubby clothing and a wig. My boobs were compressed against my chest. The curves I'd enjoyed had shriveled because there wasn't much to eat here. How his gaze could hold admiration was beyond me.

"Don't look at me that way," I said, wishing my voice came out stronger.

"You've changed, Charlie."

"Time does that to a person."

Frowning, he stabbed his fingers through his hair. It

was a wonder he didn't slice it all off with his thumb claw. "You look—"

Shouts rang out in the hall, and dismay widened his eyes.

Adrenaline spiked my pulse into overdrive. My palms became clammy.

"Great," I snapped. "You need to hide, Shaede."

He shoved open the door, grabbed my hand, and hustled me into the hall. "Just stay behind me."

I'd never remain behind any male, not even a hot one like him.

Two guards rushed toward us, and a glance over my shoulder showed five more coming from the opposite direction. I could handle two alone. Seven might present a challenge.

"Maybe you should remain behind me," I said, shouldering past him to run toward the closest guards.

I'd intended to slink across the wasteland once I'd figured out what was going on here, not stomp my way out with my fists. Leave it to Shaede to decide my fate once again.

Shaede spun to challenge the guys coming from the other direction, his thick horns slicing through the air. As I swept one of the guard's feet out from beneath him and landed a solid hit to the other's solar plexus, I caught Shaede leaping, barreling into the other guards like a ball hitting pins. They tangled together and crashed to the stone floor.

My fellow inmates clung to the bars of their cells,

most watching silently, a few cheering me and Shaede on. None rooted for the guards.

"What you doing?" My friend, Pralk, asked from his cell, concern lighting up his voice.

I didn't have time to reply.

Using my favorite move, I grabbed the necks of the two I battled and brought their heads together, taking in the satisfying crack they made when they connected. The lizard aliens slumped, and I turned in time to see two guards out of commission but the other three holding Shaede down while messing up his pretty face.

I wasn't sure why I cared about them leaving bruises, except a soft feeling still lingered inside me for my older brother's best friend. I'd tried to stomp the feeling into oblivion, but a tiny flame still flickered.

"Run," he cried, struggling to break free of the guards.

I snarled and leaped toward them, hitting the chest of a particularly tall, gray skinned Vessar guard. We tumbled to the floor, but lizards were not only cunning, but they also got slippery when angry, their scaly skin secreting an oil that made them extra hard to hold on to. We grappled, but my hands kept sliding across his skin.

In no time, I lay beneath him, never a treat considering Vessar claws, pointed-tip tails, and vicious teeth.

He hauled me up as the other two wrangled with Shaede. Shaede's bellows turned to grunts that muted to silence. My guts were wrenched sideways by fear.

The Vessar dragged me across Shaede's still body. He tossed me into my cell, and I slammed against the wall above my bunk, dropping onto the equally hard surface that still held my warmth.

The guard locked my door and grabbed Shaede's bag before stomping over to the others.

I slid off the bunk, chomping my teeth on the groan eager to escape. I'd hurt my right leg when I hit the wall, but I couldn't let on that I was injured. A thing like that would be seen as weakness, and inside a prison, weakness spiraled into a quick death.

A guard hefted Shaede's leg. Shaede didn't move or respond, making me worry he was dead. My heart curled into a tight ball at the thought of a galaxy without him.

He'd devastated me six yaros ago. He didn't deserve a speck of my pity, let alone something bordering close to affection.

While the inmates around me slunk back to their bunks, the guards stomped down the hall, dragging Shaede across the stone floor behind them.

CHAPTER TWO
SHAEDE

I dreamed of Charlie creeping over to where I lay. She knelt beside me and touched my forehead with her warm fingers.

Something scurried nearby, its claws tapping on the floor, but I didn't open my eyes. I wanted to remain within the dream, because here, Charlie still cared.

"Jeez, Shaede, what did they do to you?" she said. Funny how exasperation came through in her voice even when she was just a fantasy.

Because I had some control over this dream, I'd have her fulfill everything I'd ever wished for.

She tentatively stroked along my jaw to my neck, and her gasp rang out. "You're still wearing the pendant I gave you."

It was the only connection I still had with her, and I'd never take it off.

Water dimly splashed, and her fingers were replaced

by a damp cloth. She wiped my face, grumbling about bruises.

The cloth continued down my neck to the top of my shirt.

"Leave it to you to try to rescue me and get captured yourself," she huffed. "What am I going to do with you?"

I had a few ideas, ones that had simmered for the six long yaros after she told me she liked me. After she asked me to kiss her.

There wasn't anything I'd wanted to do more, but she was my best friend's younger sister. Some boundaries weren't meant to be crossed, especially with a sweet, vulnerable female like Charlie.

But this was a dream, so I could give into my endless need for the female she'd grown into, right?

I took the cloth from her and tossed it aside. A tug, and she lay across my chest. I liked her there, with her thighs spread around my hips. She braced her palms on my shoulders, and I didn't imagine her stroking me through the thick fabric of my shirt.

"What are you doing, Shaede?" she asked, skeptical.

At twenty-four to her eighteen, I'd been too experienced for an innocent like her. I wasn't sure why six yaros passing should make a difference, but it did.

The innocence was gone from her eyes, but the Charlie I'd crushed on even back then remained.

When her brother sent word that she'd been stolen and taken to the Vessar prison, there wasn't anything I wouldn't do to save her. I told him I'd handle it, then I'd pretty much gone AWOL, telling my boss I had something I needed to take care of. I hadn't waited for his reply.

Another quick twist, and she lay beneath me, staring up at me with her lips parted and her heels hitched on my hips.

"Shaede, you shouldn't—"

I stole her words, her lips, her everything, claiming this female with one long kiss. It was everything I'd dreamed of back when I chastised myself for watching the sway of Matis's seventeen-year-old sister's hips. I'd wanted her, and my friend would've been right to smack me for my impertinent thoughts.

Back then, I'd behaved. I'd kept my hands and lips to myself.

Now? Dream Charlie lay beneath me, and I was taking what I'd ached to possess all those yaros ago.

A moan escaped her lips, and her arms tightened on my shoulders, pulling me down on top of her.

What they'd done to her was a crime. She'd been lush and curvy, and they'd stolen that from her. Starved her!

And her glorious, wonderful auburn hair. How had they turned it black? She'd cut it, which was also a crime, but females had the right to do what they wanted with their own bodies. Yet I hated seeing her gorgeous tresses gone.

My fingers traced up her side and beneath her loose shirt, and I frowned when I found something strapped across her chest.

Her lips broke away from mine, and she glared. "What are you doing?"

"Kissing you."

"You don't want to kiss me."

"Seems like I do, since I was just doing it." This was a dream. It had to be a dream. But why was dream-Charlie arguing with me?

Leave it to me to grab onto a dream where we still had an adversarial relationship, not the sweet friendship we'd shared until she told me she liked me.

Back then, I'd run, not stopping until I'd put a galaxy between us.

She bucked her hips. "Let me go."

I rolled off her. "Not holding you down, sweetheart." Though I wanted to. I wanted to take her hands and pin them over her head. Then start kissing her again, not stopping until I'd made her cry out my name.

She slid off the bunk and scooted through the cell door, pulling it shut behind her. A small blue creature scowled at me before following her, slipping between the bars.

I fell back on the bunk and rubbed my eyes.

When I looked toward the door of my cell, she was gone, proving it had just been a dream.

CHAPTER THREE
CHARLIE

It was all I could do not to bang my cell door shut behind me. But if the guards discovered I could pick it open, they'd make sure I never got out again.

Why had I gone to Shaede?

Because I was worried. I was scared he was dead. It would've killed me if I never saw him again.

Instead, I'd straddled him, let him roll me beneath him. Allowed him to kiss me.

Was I truly the same needy girl I'd been back when I was eighteen?

Maybe.

No, my conscience said. *We're over him.*

Sure, the little voice on my left shoulder said with a snicker.

"Shut up," I whispered.

Damn, I hated when I argued with parts of myself.

I dropped down onto my bunk and pulled up the blanket. Rosie joined me, perching on my chest. She scowled as if she wanted to chastise me for going to Shaede.

"You're right," I said, stroking her fur. "I should've stayed here."

Her little head whipped to the hall outside my cell. With a cheep, she dove beneath the blankets. I closed my eyes and snorted like I was deep asleep.

"You isss awake," someone hissed from my cell door, making me grateful all over again I'd made sure the lock engaged when I stepped inside. "Awakesss," Warden Gruxidon snarled. "We talksss."

Yeah, sure. The last time someone "talked" with him, the guy ended up with his skull bashed in.

When I first arrived, I was determined to escape as soon as possible. I didn't intend on making friends, but a few had wormed their way into my heart. I hadn't known the guy the warden callously killed, but I lived in fear he'd hurt one of my friends.

I could snort and pretend I was still sleeping, but if the warden wanted a conversation, he wasn't above entering my cell and slamming me against the wall to make sure I paid attention. I liked my skull un-bashed and my skin unbruised.

If I hadn't found a vein of brugeer within dias of my arrival, I'd probably be dead.

The first time he'd questioned me about the brugeer, he'd behaved in a civilized manner, calling me to his office. I'd survived only because he thought being "kind," would result in me sharing the location of the drug he and the other Vessars craved.

The second time, he'd cast off any pretense of kindness and chained me to a wall. If one of the guards hadn't notified him that a new crop of prisoners had arrived, he would've peeled back my layers and revealed all my secrets. No one could hold up under torture forever. He would've killed me once he got the information.

"Where isss vein?" he snarled, raking his claws down the bars with a sharp squeal.

When I was suspended in front of him, my arms almost sucked from their sockets, he'd punctuated this very same question with a poke of a claw in my side that took five dias to heal.

"If I tell you, I'm no longer useful," I said softly to keep the guards from overhearing. If they thought he'd take it all, I wasn't sure what they'd do. Probably kill me.

"Why no othersss find brugeer beneath planet'sss surface?" Warden Gruxidon asked in a low voice, his claws stilling.

"Maybe they lack the same incentive as me." I remained on my bunk, pretending a nonchalance I didn't feel.

Poor Rosie trembled. He scared her, with good reason.

He slammed his fists on the bars. "Other inmatesss wantsss favorsss too."

"I'm sure they do." Giving up on sleep, I swung my legs off my bunk, dangling them. "Tell you what. Make sure I have extra rations today, and I'll see what I can do to bring you more brugeer."

"Three timesss amount," he growled, his fingers curling around the bars.

"Two. You know it's not easy to extract brugeer from solid rock." I held up my hands, displaying the nicks and cuts I'd received from working in the mine over the past thirty-one dias. "Look at me. I'm all beat up. It's all I can do to get two buckets of brugeer out of the ground."

"Restsss. Then getsss more."

"Kind of hard to rest with you scowling at me." Over the past dias, I'd gone from being terrified my identity would be discovered and I'd be killed for being a former interstellar agent, to a cocky behavior that hadn't sunk beneath my skin. I'd sensed acting like I was in control—when I wasn't—would be the best way to get what I needed.

I needed food to share with those in solitary.

And I needed to discover what was going on here before I fled.

Now I could add Shaede to the mix. Before we escaped, I'd need to obtain more water and food. More credits. Another set of clothing, though I supposed we could cross the wasteland in the outfits we escaped in.

Could I double my production and secret it away in my escape tunnel? Then I could trade brugeer for one-way tickets off this planet.

At this rate, I'd be digging beneath the ground for the rest of my life.

Who would've thought I'd fall from my lofty enforcement position to that of a drug dealer?

Mostly. Brugeer only worked on Vessars and at best,

it made them feel silly, much like marijuana used to do back in Earth's past. It may be non-addictive, but they still craved the escape it brought, a welcome break from a prison.

"Do it. Three bucketsss." The warden's muscles bulged as he shook the bars, and it was a scarily impressive sight to see bits of ceiling falling to the stone floor from his efforts. "Or elsesss."

He turned as if to leave but glared over his shoulder. "If I not leavesss for dias, I would makesss you."

Leaving for a few dias? While he was gone, I'd finish this job and flee across the wasteland.

"I makesss you," he repeated, threat alive in his voice. His growl ripped out of him, and he fumbled with the master key attached to a thin chain at his waist.

But when he started to open my door, something hit him on the back of his head.

As he whirled around, my gaze shot to Pralk lying still on his bunk in the cell opposite mine. He snorted, but I could tell he wasn't asleep. My friend had distracted the warden. Would he pay the price Gruxidon had been determined to take from my flesh?

Warden Gruxidon stormed over to Pralk's cell, but he only glared through the barred door.

He turned back to me and snarled, but instead of following through on his threat, he strode down the aisle between the cells. The door at the end of the hall banged shut as he left.

My shaking hands were the only sign of the anxiety

bolting through me. I remained motionless until I was confident the warden wouldn't return.

"You take many chancesss," Pralk whispered from his bunk.

"I'm sorry."

He sighed. "Work in minesss. Sleepsss. Eatsss. Nothing else."

I pinched my eyes shut. There was no way I'd resign myself to a life here. I'd finish the job I fell into and escape, though I'd do all I could to help my friends along the way.

"I'll be careful." It was all I was able to say. "You need to be careful too. Don't do that again." It would gut me if the warden hurt my friend.

"Do as pleasesss," Pralk grunted. He rolled over, facing away from me.

It was a mistake to care for fellow inmates.

On my first day here, Pralk told me I reminded him of his younger brother, that he was going to make sure I survived the prison—unlike his younger brother. How could I turn my back on someone who made sure I had enough to eat, who helped fill my buckets if I got behind, and who intervened with the warden whenever he could?

Caring created complications, but I was going to make sure I wasn't the only one who escaped this trap. I just had to figure out how I'd do it.

Prisoners shifted around me. Had they heard the warden's words? I'd have to grow eyes on the back of my head. Many would kill to learn where I'd found the brugeer. Then they could claim the vein for themselves, using it to manipulate the warden for favors. Without my secret stash, I'd be back to hard labor extracting gems, too tired at the end of the dia to dream about escape, let alone scour the prison for secrets.

Rising, I started pacing.

It was time to figure out what was going on here and get out. Hopefully, Shaede would recover soon and be able to flee beside me under his own steam.

If not, I'd drag him behind me.

Because we'd be stupid to remain here much longer.

CHAPTER FOUR
SHAEDE

Eyes open and my body on fire, I stared around the tiny cell where the guards had dumped me.

Had Charlie been here? It wasn't possible. Yet my lips still felt hot from our kiss. My bunk was warm from her body.

And . . . I peered over the side. Yes, *there*. The cloth lay on the floor where she'd dropped it.

She had been here, and we'd kissed. She'd writhed beneath me with true passion.

There might be hope for us yet.

My rueful snort shot out. Hope for us? If I was lucky, I'd live long enough to see her again. At this point, I was surprised they hadn't taken me somewhere for questioning. Maybe they were waiting for me to wake up. If I was wise, I'd pretend I hadn't.

Eyes closed and my body motionless, I allowed sleep to claim me once more.

I sunk into another dream where Charlie and I lay in

deep grass, staring up at the stars. Her hair was auburn once more, and her body full and curvy, just the way I remembered. Physical appearance wasn't everything. If it was, the scar slicing halfway down the right side of my face would be enough to scare her away.

But if I was going to dream about Charlie, why not the one I remembered combined with the assertive, confident Charlie I'd met here at the prison?

Holding her hand, I pointed to a star spiking across the sky.

"Where do you think it's going?" she asked, her fingers meshing with mine.

Like I'd done earlier, and like I'd wanted but hadn't dared to do when she was eighteen, I rolled over and braced myself above her.

"It's soaring into your heart," I said.

"That's sweet, which totally isn't you, Shaede."

Even dream Charlie had a cheeky mouth. I liked it. Adored it as much as I did her. Six yaros felt like nothing, as if we'd stepped off the page for a short break only to step back into the book and take up where we'd left off.

This time, if she told me she liked me, I wouldn't nudge her away.

Her lips curled up slyly, and my hearts soared like the stars. She was everything and all I would ever need.

I kissed her, claiming her mouth. Branding her as mine.

She moaned as I trailed my fingers up her side. This time, nothing stopped me from touching her. Stroking her. Her nipple tightened beneath my fingers. I'd claim that soon too—every bit of this female who'd haunted me for yaros.

My cock surged upward. Nothing would make me happier than to sink myself inside her and ride her until we were both moaning wrecks. No, until she whimpered and called out my name.

But this was a dream, the one that had visited me almost nightly since I turned away from the soft excitement in her eyes. I'd tried to drown that look since we parted in both rezin and welcome females, but both tasted bitter, like I'd had the chance at the most decadent treat and tossed it aside. Everything else became a pale imitation.

It wasn't easy to tell someone you liked them, but she'd done it, sharing her feelings in a shy, sweet way.

Some guys would've taken what she offered. I'd been tempted. But I'd worried I was taking advantage of her and my friendship with her brother. I told myself I didn't want to ruin what me and Matis had, what me and Charlie had. If it didn't work out, things would be awkward between us.

Fool that I was, I made it worse. I turned and walked away, ignoring her whimper of dismay. I regretted turning her down, but there was no way I could take what she'd offered. A guy with a background like mine would never deserve such a sweet, lovely female like Charlie.

"Shaede," she whispered, her fingers playing down my spine. "Shaede."

"I'm sorry, Charlie," I said, repeating the words I'd

mumbled to myself every dia since I walked out of her life. "I wish . . ."

Wishes would never come true for a male like me.

"Don't wish," she said, her form turning to mist. Only her words remained. "If you want something, you need to take it, not dream about it."

I woke suddenly to a pounding head and a bitter taste in my mouth. The first came from one of the guards slamming my skull against the stone floor. The second must come from whatever they'd injected me with after they dragged me into this cell.

A quick glance showed I lay on a bunk like Charlie's, locked within the prison.

The cloth on the floor drew my eye.

How had she gotten here? If she could slip from her cell, why hadn't she escaped already?

Something was going on here, and I was determined to find out what it was. Well, once I'd gotten out of this cell and tracked her down again.

I reached for the slender chain I'd tucked inside my shirt and fingered the pendant. Charlie gave it to me the holiday before I broke her heart, and I'd worn it ever since. Had she seen it last night?

Would it matter if she knew I'd worn it all these yaros?

I sat up on the side of the bunk and rubbed the back of my head, finding a lump, though no broken skin. My horns jutting up across my head had protected my skull many times in the past, and they'd done so again last night.

"Up. Go," a guard said, banging the side of his zapper on my cell door.

"Go where?"

"Time to worksss," he hissed.

"I'm not an inmate." I wasn't exactly sure what I was now, however. Perhaps being caught sneaking in was all it took to be incarcerated here for life.

Foolish me had told only Matis where I was going.

Did Charlie know her brother had infiltrated a space pirate operation? He was undercover, on assignment, which meant I had to handle this situation on my own.

The guard gouged the zapper between the bars, shooting a jolt of electricity into my knee. "Up."

Fire blasted down my leg, and my toes went numb. I leapt to my feet, and a growl ripped from my throat. I flexed my hands, aching to rip my thumb claws across his throat. "I'm not an inmate."

"Aresss prisoner now," he said. I took in his long snout with his alligator-like jaws full of sharp teeth. "Wantsss in prison? Isss in." His hand snapped out, grabbing my wrist, and he hauled me against the bars. If my foot functioned correctly, I wouldn't have stumbled. No, he would've tasted my fist against his mouth. But it didn't matter when he snapped a restraint around my wrist. "Other handsss." His glare took in my right side.

Fighting someone through bars when he held the weapon was never a smart idea. I needed to save my strength for the chance that would come. The minue I saw it, I'd take it and run.

But only with Charlie by my side.

After he'd secured my wrists, leaving only a short distance between them, he unlocked the door and hauled me through the opening. Again, I didn't fight him, and my passive behavior was rewarded when he opted to stuff the second restraint back into his pocket rather than apply it to my ankles.

"Comesss," he said, shuffling down the hall, his tail spiking up to lay against his spine. The tip curled back toward me. I wasn't stupid. Vessars had eerie senses and knew when someone was about to attack. His tail could thrust backward and kill me with two thrusts through my chest, one for my first heart before he yanked it out and stabbed it back in to take out the second.

The guard stopped at other cells to collect all the inmates in this wing, linking us together, but none of the cells contained Charlie.

Was she all right?

Matis was going to kill me. Though our communication was limited, when he reached out about Charlie, I'd promised I'd get his sister out of here and back home in no time.

I wasn't giving up yet.

We turned a corner, and partway down the hall, the guard released Charlie.

Her gaze noted me shuffling among the mix, and her lips thinned. Her eyes flashed something I couldn't define before she turned to stride unrestrained ahead of the guard.

What made her rate any different from the rest of us?

There was something odd about her, and it wasn't just her flattened shape. Her hair . . .

Was she wearing a wig over her gorgeous auburn hair? That, her frame, and the loose, dingy clothing made her look like a youngling of about seventeen, and that must be the point.

How in all the fates could anyone miss the female walking in their midst?

Maybe Vessars and the other species here hadn't seen many humans.

Her pretty green eyes held the same stiffness I'd earned when she was eighteen. It had resided there last night when I opened her cell to rescue her. They didn't smolder with chained heat like they had when I cradled her beneath me and fused our mouths together in a kiss that still made my cock ache.

I began to believe our kiss hadn't happened. My head injury could be worse than I thought. I'd imagined the entire thing. That had to be it. I was healing, but last night . . . To say I was disappointed was an understatement.

One of the inmates stumbled into me, reminding me I needed to keep my mind on what was going on around me, not daydream about Charlie.

They marched us from the lower level of the prison, up two flights of stairs, and to a big open room. We shuffled down a line where they gave each of us a bowl of watery gruel.

"Eatsss," one of the guards lounging against the wall by the door shouted. "Goesss soon."

We drank our breakfast fast.

Charlie watched me while eating her own meal. Finished, she dropped her bowl onto a table lining the left wall and stepped out into the hall, still unbound.

The guards hustled the rest of us out into the yard, where skimmers waited with open hatches. Once they'd loaded us on board, the vehicles lifted off and soared over the enormous wall, leaving the main prison compound behind.

I studied the razor spikes lining the top of the wall with a narrow passage between them where guards strolled, plus the wall's height. There'd be no jumping over the wall and even if I could climb it without being shot by someone watching from the top, it would be a challenge to get past the razors. The green-coated tips suggested poison. One nick, and I'd be dead before I hit the ground on the other side.

The skimmers soared across a big open stretch made up of muddy water, small mounds of scrubby soil, and a few spindly trees. The murky water bubbled. Each cluster of air indicated a creature lurking beneath the surface, waiting for someone to stumble past.

Three nights ago, I'd hidden my small ship in the forest on the opposite side of the wasteland. It took two nights to cross the sand and mud-covered stretch between the forest and the prison, and while it had been a treacherous crossing, I was eager to grab Charlie and traverse it again.

Assuming I could find Charlie. I hadn't seen her since she left the breakfast room.

The skimmers aimed for a series of hills far in the distance, and it took a while to reach the spiky chain of mountains.

They landed the skimmers at the base of an enormous cliff and urged us to get out. Since five of us were linked together inside each vehicle, it wasn't easy. We eventually stood together while one group was sorted out from the rest.

This quiet group of prisoners didn't look our way as the guards spoke to them in low voices. Their clothing was relatively clean and unworn compared to everyone else.

Guards handed them bundles of food and flasks of water.

Males around me grumbled, making me wonder if the watery gruel would be my only meal of the dia.

Two of the guards led the small group of prisoners along the cliff. They reached the right end and disappeared around the side.

Would all of us be divided into small groups and taken somewhere? The lack of additional food and water for us suggested the first group was special. I could think of a variety of reasons to coerce prisoners into doing something for you, but I couldn't pin any of them down yet. Nowhere near enough information.

And I wasn't here to uncover prison planet secrets. I needed to locate Charlie and get us out of here.

"What's going on?" I softly asked the Vessar crouched beside me.

His long tail flicked back and forth behind him,

brushing the ground as he turned his pointy snout my way. Most Vessars walked upright, but some hadn't evolved enough to support their weight on their hind legs. This created a pecking order among the lizards, with those moving on four legs relegated to the bottom of the pack.

"Themsss?" the Vessar hissed like they all did. "Do not knowsss. Always themsss. Go in first. More food. Different work. Usss? Enter minesss soon. Work hard. Eat later maybe."

"Mines?" I squinted toward the cave entrances peppering the side of the cliff.

"We entersss there." He jutted a clawed hand toward the first cave entrance. "Go into ground." His hind legs shifted, moving his considerable bulk onto his far-right leg. "We digsss. Collectsss. Bring bucketsss up and go back for more."

"What are we mining?" I asked. It wasn't that odd to put prisoners to work, though I doubt we'd be paid with more than food, and not much of that.

"Gemsss."

That made sense. They'd fetch a high price on the interstellar market. No matter where you went in this galaxy and the ones surrounding it, there were people eager to buy stones and turn them into something to wear or, perhaps, a figurine to sit on a shelf. If you were very wealthy, you might line the inner walls of your home with jewels. The demand never diminished.

One of the guards went through the rest of the prisoners, unlinking us. They also shackled my ankles, giving me just enough space to walk but not run. The cord connecting our wrists were extended to give us more movement.

"Get to worksss," a Vessar guard snarled. "Three bucketsss gemsss."

My fellow prisoners groaned.

"Two yesterdaysss," the male beside me said softly. "*Two.* That challenge enough. This job sucksss." Grumbling, he stumbled over to a bin full of tools and grabbed some before shuffling to a path weaving up the face of the cliff.

I followed, sorting quickly through the bin and selecting a pick, a bucket, and a blast hammer. Our goal was to find big chunks of rock containing gemstones. Masters would extract the gems from the rock and cut them into jewels to be sold for a pretty price at the market.

When I started up the path to the mine opening, a commotion behind me sent me spinning.

Another skimmer approached, landing near the others. The hatch opened, and Charlie hopped out.

The Vessar guards looked her way and cheered.

CHAPTER FIVE
CHARLIE

I was no celebrity, but I'd been slipping the guards nuggets of brugeer each time I brought a full bucket out of the mine—carefully, that is. In exchange, they made sure the creepiest prisoners were assigned to different underground passages, and that I had water and food, most of which I secreted away when the rest weren't looking. At first, I'd used it to create caches all over the place, waiting for me to grab them when I fled, but over the past half a lunar cycle, I'd shared it with my friends.

I wasn't sure what the guards would do after what happened the night before, but when I strolled over to them, they all grinned. Maybe this group was unaware of my actions or maybe they didn't want to create waves and miss out on their share of brugeer.

Vessars loved how brugeer made them feel, and who wouldn't want to feel silly if they were stuck working on a sucky planet prison? If only the stuff worked on humans.

"How's it goin'?" I asked the guards, shifting my shirt at the waist where Rosie hid. From the first dia, she'd refused to remain in my cell while I worked. Scared someone would kill her, I'd started hiding her inside my clothing until I was hidden inside the tiny cave where I'd located the vein of brugeer.

"Mine," one said with a growl, pushing me. So much for my claim to fame. "Bringsss brugeer."

At first, I'd believed brugeer was the secret here, but a few overheard whispers suggested something bigger—and badder—was going on. Time was running out, however. I needed to decide if I dared to remain here long enough to unveil the secret or if I should cut my losses and flee.

Shaede complicated my self-imposed assignment. Speaking of the guy who'd broken my heart, where was he? Maybe already inside the mine unless they'd opted to leave him in his cell.

Hopefully, he wasn't being held for questioning by the warden, though there wasn't much I could do for him if he was.

Pralk watched as I grabbed buckets and tools, strapped on a headlamp, and started up the path.

"What you doing?" he hissed, walking in front of me. "Try escapesss last night?"

"Wouldn't you, given the chance?"

He grunted in agreement. "Who other guy?"

"A . . . friend. He thinks he came to rescue me."

Pralk snorted. "Badsss rescue."

"Yeah."

"Lucky Warden leavesss for dias. Otherwise . . ." He made a slicing motion across his throat.

No matter how I felt about Shaede, I would keep that from happening. The clock was ticking. I had to discover what was going on here and flee. "Have you heard where they're keeping my friend?"

"He here."

I peered around but didn't see him anywhere. Maybe he was already inside the mine.

We reached the top of the cliff, and I followed Pralk to the mine entrance, my step only faltering when I spied Shaede waiting in the shade of the cave opening.

After slipping from his cell and gathering my wits together after our spine-tingling kiss, I'd spent half the night awake.

I'd worried his injuries were worse than I'd thought.

I'd worried he'd be dead by morning.

I'd worried the warden would haul him to the interrogation room and chain him to the wall.

Pralk glanced back and forth between us before striding into the cave opening and down the slope leading into the depths of the mountains.

I followed, and Shaede fell in behind me as cool air engulfed me, skating across my exposed skin.

I shook off a shiver and switched on my headlamp, keeping it muted to allow my eyes to adjust to the growing darkness.

My fellow inmates moved around us, their buckets

clanking against their sides and their lights spearing stone walls as they strode into various tunnels. We all worked in different areas to keep from stumbling over each other and to protect whatever vein of gems we'd discovered. I was always the last to leave the main path because I didn't want anyone else to see where I'd found brugeer.

"How's the head?" I finally asked when Shaede had remained silent for what felt like many horus.

"Pounding, but I'll survive."

My knees loosened, which irritated me, though not because I wanted to hear he was in pain. No, my feelings went farther than the sympathy of one person for another. I thought I'd stamped out my feelings for Shaede ages ago. Six yaros with no communication should've cemented them within my soul.

Kissing him, no, thrusting my hips up against his aroused cock, brought all those feelings crashing down onto me again.

Why couldn't I purge him from my heart?

"Why did you come here?" I asked as we walked down the slope that was like the trunk of a tree. I'd step into one of the branches soon, as would the rest, but once I'd traveled deeper within the mountain, I'd escape into my secret cave.

"I told you last night, I'm here to rescue you. Matis heard you were taken, and he got in touch."

"I appreciate your effort, but it wasn't necessary."

"Yet, here you are, a prisoner heading down into a mine to excavate gems."

I tapped the bucket he carried with my pick. "Yet, here we *both* are, heading into the mine to excavate gems," I said lightly. For some reason, I wasn't eager to mock him. "Why you? Matis could've sent anyone else."

"I volunteered."

"Oh, really?"

"I owe you."

His words were a blade hitting me in the chest, but I held my spine tight despite the pain.

"That's interesting," I said, pausing. I pretended to fix the hem of my pants, tucking it into the top of my boot to create a barrier to any creeping creature in the area. I also waited for the rest of the prisoners to enter passages. "I didn't realize you owed me anything."

"I could've handled it differently," he grated out, rubbing the back of his head.

"I'm not sure what you're talking about," I said, brightening my lamp to study the nearby walls.

"I should've been kinder with my . . . rejection."

Grumbling, I faced him. "Why do you think what happened eons ago matters to me?" It did, but he'd never hear it from me. "It's been six yaros. I barely remember who you are."

Consternation filled his face. "But you . . ."

"What, flung myself at you? Stood strong while you said you weren't interested? Watched you walk away while holding my head high? I did all that. And I forgot all about you not long after."

Not really. I'd broken down. Cried. Railed at the world for being so unfair.

But then I'd dried my tears and told myself no guy would ever hurt me again. I'd held that promise close and enforced it whenever someone tried to wiggle his way into my heart. Sure, I'd been with guys. I'd cared for a few of them too. But no one else had gotten past the armor plating surrounding my heart. Not like Shaede had.

"We need to work," I said, waving my hammer toward the branches exiting the main passage. "Go find some gems."

"I'll stick near you if you don't mind."

"I do mind." I'd explore the second floor of the prison tonight. The first and the ground floor held prisoners, and the top levels contained guard housing. I'd left the second floor until last since it was often occupied.

Once I'd figured out what was going on here, I'd flee. If I hit things right, I'd be partway across the wasteland within dias.

You'll take Shaede with you, my conscience piped up.

Why bother? The little, sly voice on my left shoulder snarled.

He's your brother's best friend, conscience said.

He rejected you. Give him a taste of how that feels, the other voice said.

"Shut up," I hissed, and Shaede looked at me oddly.

It was my conscience's fault I'd kissed him last night. If she hadn't kept harping about how he could be injured or dying, I would've remained in my cell and dealt with him now.

But then I wouldn't have shared my first kiss with him.

I groaned. First kiss? Last was more like it.

It would be mean to leave him behind, my niggling little conscience said.

Sly voice shrugged. *He tossed himself into the ring now didn't he?*

"Enough!" I snarled.

Shaede blinked. "Excuse me?"

"I wasn't talking to you," I said, edging around him. "Follow me." My lips compressed thinner than the paper Earthlings used to write on before tech placed written words in cyberspace.

"You lead, I'll follow, sweetheart." His voice sounded all deep and husky, implying he was here as my protector. But his tone only made my lips tighten even further.

"Jeez, don't call me that."

He just grinned.

Sighing, I continued down the slope, passing channels the rest of the inmates had taken. Bangs and buzzes echoed around us as my fellow prisoners worked hard to extract gems. The dia passed quickly when it could take you an horus to extract one decent chunk that could yield a few gems. Filling one bucket with those was a big enough assignment, let alone three.

"Wouldn't it be better to collect everything closer to the surface?" he asked, his more reasonable voice filling the silence I'd been savoring. "Less distance to carry it."

"Not what I'm mining for."

"Gems."

"That too."

He grumbled. "What's going on here, Charlie? You were greeted like a celebrity by the guards. You're not chained."

"I'm special."

He rolled his eyes. "This is a prison."

"No," I gasped. I picked up my pace, striding down the slope. "Keep up and watch closely, Shaede."

"We don't have all dia."

"We'll get what they want before it ends."

By nightfall, our hands would be stinging from being sliced by stone, and every muscle in our bodies would ache. If we were lucky, we wouldn't emerge into the light with fractures. Too often, the walls or ceiling would collapse around us, burying a few who were soon replaced with new ones. The Vessars weren't big on supplying supporting structures to keep us safe, and it wasn't like we could report them to the interstellar safety groups.

"I'm the best at finding brugeer," I whispered. "Everyone thinks I randomly came across a big source, but I studied geology at the interstellar academy. It was mostly a hobby, but one that has come in handy here."

"Ah." He studied my face, and I didn't like how judgy he appeared. "Vessars love the drug."

"Indeed."

"And you're their dealer."

I also didn't like the scorn coming through in his voice. It grated across my skin like the roughest stone.

"Don't judge, Shaede," I said.

"Not even thinking of it."

I shook my head. "I've got an ulterior motive."

"Beyond keeping the guards happy?"

"That too."

He kept walking down the slope. I stopped and bent over the tuck to my pants into the top of my boot again.

I frowned as I peered all around, making sure no one remained in the main passage.

When Shaede continued around a corner, disappearing from view, I patted Rosie, who remained hidden and quiet.

I ducked behind a large boulder blocking the right side of the path and dropped onto my hands and knees.

"Charlie?" Shaede called out in a low voice, returning to where I'd left the path.

I didn't say anything. I didn't give away my location.

He needed to go fill his buckets with gems.

No, he needed to forget all about me.

If only I could forget about him.

CHAPTER SIX

SHAEDE

She was there one minue, then gone the next. I went back to where I'd last seen her and scoured the area. I'd just started to peer behind a large boulder on the side of the path when a guard appeared at the top of this part of the slope.

"Worksss," he snarled, stabbing out with his zapper, hitting my side.

Electricity shot through me, stunning me, though not knocking me out. He must have it set to the lowest frequency.

"Find gemsss." He kicked my stacked buckets before striding down the slope, leaving me still twitching against the boulder.

It frustrated me that I couldn't find Charlie but wandering around looking for her would only result in more punishment.

Taking my tools, I did as the guard demanded, though I remained in the area where I'd last seen her, working a cluster of gems I located in the back corner of a narrow passage on the left side of the slope.

I brought my third bucket to the surface just in time to see Charlie climb into a skimmer. She stared out the window as the craft lifted, and when her gaze met mine, I swore I read sorrow on her face.

I had to be imagining things. She was angry with me, and it was going to take more than an apology to make things right between us.

***

"You're not disappearing on me today," I snarled at "breakfast" the next morning. I used the term loosely, since all that was offered was a mug of undercooked grains floating in gray water.

Other prisoners stood around us, some scratching parts they should leave untouched outside the dark of night, others eating quickly.

Charlie upended her cup, draining it before licking her lips. "Allow me to commend the chef. Excellent dish. Excellent."

Her joke brought out my smile, but it disappeared as I stared at the gruel in my mug.

I drank the liquid, grimacing at the musty taste, and swallowed most of the grains whole. It was food, and I'd need my strength not only to survive but to escape this trap. All they'd given us last night was dried out bread and more gruel.

"Where did you go yesterday?" I growled, swiping my hand across my lips after finishing my meal.

"I worked in the mines, bringing out three buckets, and let me tell you, it was tough work," she said in a perky voice. At least she'd slept. I'd spent the night lying on my bunk, hoping she'd visit my waking dream again. This time, I wouldn't let her go until I got answers to my numerous questions.

"You went somewhere. I looked for you but didn't find you."

"The mines are twisty places. I'm sure I was around somewhere."

I scowled, but before I could speak again, the guards hustled us out into the courtyard and loaded us into skimmers.

Like yesterday, Charlie rode alone and unrestrained.

The skimmer I rode in landed near hers, and we all got out.

Again, a separate group of prisoners were given food and water and escorted around the side of the cliff, presumably to work in a different mine.

I remained beside Charlie.

"Three bucketsss," the head guard said, waving his zapper toward a pile of them and the bin of tools they'd take from us at the end of the dia.

The others grabbed what they needed and trudged up the slope toward the cave entrance.

I followed Charlie and mimicked her actions, taking the same tools and three buckets, then remaining close to her as she started up the hill toward the openings. I was so close, we could be connected at the ankle.

The wrist might be better.

To keep track of this female, I might need to handcuff her to my side.

CHAPTER SEVEN

CHARLIE

"You're not disappearing on me again," Shaede said.

"I told you. I was just working, like you." I strode ahead of him, down the slope and into the mine.

Other prisoners stomped along with us. A few peeled off the path, taking channels on one side or another. Most chose to work closer to the surface. As Shaede said, why labor deep below the ground when you had to carry your buckets back out?

But good stuff could be found in the most unlikely locations.

This time, when I stopped and bent down to tuck my pants into the top of my boot, Shaede halted with me.

"We're not attached at the hip," I grumbled. How could I sneak away when he was watching?

"Maybe we are."

I rolled my eyes. "Get to work. It takes quite a long time to fill three buckets."

"Of gems, yes. I'm not sure it takes you long to collect three buckets of brugeer."

"Then find some brugeer and start collecting it yourself."

"Only if you do it with me."

"What do you think, Rosie?" I asked the palm-sized creature hiding in my shirt.

She stuck her little nose out from beneath the fabric and chittered.

Shaede's eyes widened. "What . . .?"

"Rosie? Meet Shaede. Shaede? This is my friend, Rosie."

He grinned and held out his fingers toward her.

She delicately sniffed them before chirping.

"I guess she wants me to let you in on my secret," I said.

"You got that from her cheep?"

"It was as plain as dia," I said with a roll of my eyes. "Don't you understand when she's speaking?"

He shook his head. "Show me what you're talking about."

Like the day before, I peered around, waiting for this part of the passage to clear before I scooted around the boulder and dropped to my hands and knees. Used to the routine, Rosie hopped out of my shirt and scurried ahead of me.

"Do you have to pee?" he asked snidely, moving around the side of the boulder.

"Yeah, don't watch."

He huffed.

"You just want a peek at my ass," I said.

"Always, sweetheart."

"Don't call me that."

He grinned. "Pull your pants down, now, and be quick about it."

"Guys have it so good. You can haul it out, wave it around to mark the wall and ceiling for all I know, then tuck it back. One quick fastening, and you're as good as new. Women need to haul our pants down to our ankles, squat, and cringe while it splatters our shins."

"You take all the mystery out of our differences."

"Look away, then."

"Not for a secunda." He dropped to his hands and knees beside me. "Are we mining something on the ground?"

I heaved a sigh. "Follow me." I scooted into the tiny passage Rosie had already taken with him on my tail.

He grumbled and snarled about his bound ankles and wrists, and I didn't blame him for that. It sucked when they used to bind me.

Pity stabbed through me, and I slowed my pace. There wasn't much more I could do to make this easier on him.

I had to drop to my belly at times and drag myself forward, and this is where my small human size came in handy.

Shaede's growls told me he wasn't savoring the tight walls surrounding him or the fact that he was within breathing distance of my feet.

I bathed more than most inside the prison, partly due

to my regular soirees through the prison at night. I'd found a big pool of warm water fed by a spring trickling through a crack in the wall. From what I could tell, no one but me knew the pool was there.

I'd made use of it to clean myself when I could. I'd yet to find a cleansing unit, and I'd begun to believe the Vessars never bathed.

"Where are we going?" Shaede gruffed.

"It's a secret."

He ground his teeth.

"A big secret." I wanted to explain but speaking while accessing my stash might reveal its location to others. As it was, a good number of inmates watched me, waiting for me to reveal where I found brugeer so they could dig it out of the wall for themselves.

It was only by chance I'd found the opening on my second day inside the mine. I'd almost asked one of the other inmates what they thought might be inside the passage before I decided to check it out alone.

It was creepy crawling through the first time. I kept expecting an alien creature to bite my head off.

Or to get stuck.

Instead, I'd found the small cave.

Brugeer only grew within a few types of rock, and that was what I'd initially sought. It took days before I located a section hiding a decent-sized vein. Instead of crowing about it, I'd extracted just enough to tempt the guards. They'd kept it to themselves at first, but like with everything here, the warden eventually found out and struck a deal with me. If I gave him the largest cut, he'd allow me to remain unchained and ensure I was fed and given enough water to survive.

I didn't trust him one bit, but I agreed to his deal. He'd use me, but I'd do the same with him.

After that, I began to build my escape stash, and I would've used it already if I hadn't overheard the warden talking to the head of the guards.

"They findsss?" Warden Gruxidon had said.

"More than we hopesss," the guard hissed.

At first, I thought they meant brugeer, but that didn't add up. If they had their own stash, why keep after me to bring them more?

Nope, I decided. They were talking about something else.

Gruxidon glanced around, not realizing I wasn't asleep in my bunk. "Good. Keepsss themsss working."

With that, he strode away.

I would've dismissed the conversation if I hadn't seen a couple of guards loading a large number of containers full of something emitting a faint glow into skimmers when I'd finished early for the dia and stood in the shadows of the cave entrance.

Many stones glowed, but only stripeene gave off pinkish light.

I'd tried to get close to the skimmer to check it out, but guards shouted for me to back off, so I did. That's when I added two and two and came up with ten. Something bigger than mining gems was going on here, and I was in the perfect position to find out.

I'd been investigating since, but I'd found no

evidence of anything but the usual stuff you'd see at a prison. Hence my sneaking out each night to look around some more. Before I fled the prison, I'd get to the bottom of whatever was going on and report my information to the proper authorities.

I crawled out of the long tunnel and flicked on my headlamp.

The room gleamed with treasure.

Standing, I grinned proudly at the thick vein of brugeer lining the far wall.

Shaede joined me, and my grin widened at his sigh of relief that he'd escaped being crushed by a mountain of rock.

"Nice," he said, approaching the wall. "This will keep the guards happy for quite some time."

"It would if I planned to extract it and bring it to them, which I don't."

"You'll need to if you want to keep them agreeable, won't you, sweetheart?"

He said it in such a know-it-all voice that I wanted to smack him. Why had I thought I liked him?

Oh, I remembered now. The sweet eighteen-yaro-old I'd buried deep inside me, the one who believed in hearts and flowers and all that junk, had liked the cute sway of this guy's narrow hips. The way his eyes gleamed when he talked about sports and foods he liked. The fact that he was kind to his best friend's younger sister hadn't hurt either. It wasn't necessarily his fault I'd taken his kindness as interest.

No matter. I wouldn't do it again.

Still, there was nothing wrong with showing him I wasn't the gullible teen who'd stared at him with stars in her eyes. I'd gone to the same interstellar academy he and Matis had. I'd run plenty of covert operations since.

Man, was he ever confident in himself. He wasn't the only one who'd had special ops training.

"I'm playing the Vessars," I said.

His head cocked. Stepping closer to the wall, he traced his finger along the thick vein. "What do you mean?"

"They love brugeer, and I give it to them as a distraction."

Turning, he leaned back against the wall, furrows creasing his thick brow. "Explain," he barked, crossing his muscular arms on his chest.

His attitude got my back up. "I don't need to tell you anything else."

"Sure, you do. I came here to rescue you, which means I'm in charge of this operation. If there's something going on other than brugeer and gem mining, you need to fill me in."

"You're a complication I don't need right now." I nudged him to the side and laid the tip of my pick on the lower edge of the brugeer where I'd excavated yesterday.

Rosie followed, hopping across the floor to huddle by the wall. She watched us with a sharpness that suggested she understood everything we said, but that wasn't possible.

A few bangs of my hammer, and a good-sized chunk of brugeer popped away from the wall, dropping onto the dirt floor with a dull thud. "You need to get to work, *sweetheart.*"

I loved watching his face go red. Okay, purple, due to his blue skin. He smacked his fists on his hips. "Tell me what's going on."

"I learned in training not to share missions with those who don't need to know."

"I came here to rescue you!"

Turning to face him, I lowered my tool. "Why?"

"Because Matis said you needed help."

I flopped back against the wall. "Matis doesn't need to worry about me. You don't either."

"We do."

My head tilted. "Do you worry like Matis does?"

He stalked toward me. Grabbing my shoulders, he pinned me against the wall. "Maybe I worry in a way Matis never will."

Danger, danger. He was doing his best to scrape off the scar patching my heart.

"We don't have time for this." My voice came out breathy. I sounded needy, and I hoped he didn't hear my heart thumping loudly.

"Not even a quick grope in the dark?"

"It's not dark."

"It wasn't dark the night before last, but I seem to remember you groping me."

My gaze shot to the pendant he wore around his neck. "Why didn't you throw it away?"

He glanced down at it. "It . . ."

"It what?"

"You came to my cell. You kissed me back."

"You're dreaming." I edged him away and stomped to the opposite wall, not turning.

"We have unfinished business," he whispered to my back. "And when the time is right, I'm going to stake my claim on you, Charlie."

"You're assuming I can be claimed."

"By the right male, you can."

Cocky. So cocky.

"It's been six yaros. I'm no longer interested," I said, hoping he didn't hear the shake in my voice.

"That's not what your lips and cute little moan told me the other night."

"I don't moan."

"Soon, I'm going to make you moan louder."

"You say this as if you think you know me, but you don't. I control my moans." Actually, I'd given them free rein. Him too. He could've done whatever he pleased, and I would've welcomed it. But that happened when I was tired, vulnerable. "And I wasn't with you the other night. You were delirious from the blow to your skull."

He chuckled again, and I turned around to face him. The intensity in his gaze was nearly my undoing. We were alone. We could do whatever we wanted here.

He shook his head, and I resisted the urge to tug away the strand of leather he'd used to secure his long, silvery hair at his nape. It was a shame to pin it back. It needed to be gliding across my naked skin.

I also wanted to trail my fingers along his neck to the collar of his shirt. To rip away his clothing and see everything he had to offer. The picture of him completely naked except for the pendant I'd given him floated through my mind.

Slow it down, sweetheart, my conscience shouted. *It's getting hot in here!*

I think she's doing just fine, the other voice said.

"Shut up," I hissed, making Shaede frown.

"We'll be out of here soon," he said. "And then I'm taking what you offered six yaros ago."

"I've withdrawn my offer." A complete lie. Even now, my body ached for his possession. Back then, I'd pretty much gotten myself off at the thought of being with him, and that dream hadn't died; it had slumbered, smoldering, while waiting for his touch to set me aflame once more.

"Please don't think you can do whatever you want with me." A sly smile curled my lips, and just this once, I savored making him uncomfortable, a payback for his rejection that still stung when it shouldn't. "I'm in control of this situation."

"I don't mind letting you take control, but know I'll do the same."

He meant sex, and I should snarl and tell him to keep his hands, lips, and cock to himself, but I couldn't, because he was right. There was something unfinished between us, and soon, we'd both call it due.

Did I dare throw myself at him again?

"What makes you think I want you?" I asked.

He stalked over to me, and I backed into the wall.

"This." He dragged his thumb claw down the pulse beating furiously in my neck. "And this." His claw tapped my chest where my breathing heaved. "And this." He traced his claw along my lips that parted at his touch. Traitorous things.

I bucked forward, making him back up. "None of that means anything."

"It will, sweetheart," he said with complete assurance. "It will."

I grumbled and tried to shrug off his words, but I couldn't do it. He was right. I wanted him as much as he appeared to now want me. But what would keep him from leaving me again once he'd had his fill?

No, I had to keep him at arm's length.

"I have a right to know what's going on here," he said, his cocky grin remaining true.

Spying Rosie by my feet, watching us, I scooped her up and nuzzled her against my throat. "I'm looking for something." That was all I was willing to say. Voices carried down here, and while I was confident no one could hear through the tiny passage, I wasn't one for taking chances.

The tip of his boot tapped on the ground. "Saying you're looking for something is not enough info. Tell me."

I picked up the chunk of brugeer and placed it in the bucket, then hefted the pick again. "Tell you what. When

I finish what I need to do, I'll include you in my flight plan."

"Tell me what you need to do."

"Don't you get it?" I hissed, tipping my head toward the tunnel. "Anyone could hear." After placing Rosie on the ground, I picked away at the wall. Another chunk of brugeer the size of my fist fell, followed by two more. I worked along the vein until I had enough to fill my first bucket. I could've brought all three down with me at once, but a girl needed sunlight every now and then. And with one bucket full in hand, I'd be able to wheedle food from the guards in exchange for a sample. Sometimes, I could collect supplies with each bucket.

I'd give food and water to Pralk for those who miss out on the evening meal because they hadn't been able to fill their buckets. Some of the inmates were old or injured. They couldn't keep up, but that didn't mean they should die.

"Tell me something, sweetheart," Shaede said, taking the pick from my hands.

Scowling, I lifted the full bucket. "What's with the endearment, anyway?"

He looked pensive. "Maybe you're sweet."

"I am, but you weren't interested in a sample six yaros ago."

He nudged me against the wall, and despite my determination to maintain my solid front, my hands trembled. He stroked a band of auburn hair back across my cheek, tickling my skin. It must've slipped from my wig. My distraction with him would make me break my cover. "You were eighteen. Practically a youngling. There was no way I could take what you offered."

I lifted my chin. "What's changed now?"

"Both of us, Charlie." His low, husky voice swirled through me like melted caramel. Sweet and decadent, like Shaede. "We're not the same people we were back then."

Because I didn't want him to see how flustered he made me, I urged him away and reached for my bucket again.

"How did you escape your cell the night before last?" he asked.

My fingers paused on the handle, and I didn't look his way. "I didn't."

"I could swear it was you beneath me on that bunk." He frowned. "Or some female."

Fury heated my face. "*Some* female? Who the hell do you think you—"

His chuckle broke through my jealous rage. "It *was* you. Admit it. And while you're at it, admit you enjoyed lying beneath me."

I abandoned the bucket and stormed across the tiny space that was nowhere big enough for expressing anger. "I didn't."

"I could prove it."

My gasp rang out. "You wouldn't."

"Watch me, sweetheart."

"I'm not your sweetheart."

He released a satisfied grin that made my spine twitch. "We'll see."

"I need to bring the bucket up and fetch an empty one," I said, dropping to my knees to crawl through the tunnel. "Come on, Rosie." I scooped her up and placed her inside my shirt. "You should wait here, Shaede."

He rolled his gorgeous eyes. "I'm at your back, not cowering in a tiny cave."

"I don't need protection."

"From where I'm standing, you do."

A growl ripped from me. "I told you I'm in control of the situation."

"And I told you I'm here to get you out of this prison."

"Under my terms." I shoved the bucket into the passage, planning to follow.

"Why are you still inside the prison when you can go wherever you please?"

"I have reasons." Was he going to keep me here all day asking one question after another?

You're running, my conscience said.

Stay and beg for kisses, the sly voice chimed in.

I huffed and ignored them. They were both right. I was running, and I did want to beg for kisses, neither of which I planned to do.

"Six yaros of interstellar police duty can change a person," he said, watching my every move. "If anyone knows that, it's me."

I glanced at him before tucking my head into the opening. "Confession time, Shaede?"

"Just saying," he called out, his footsteps telling me he was following. "We'll escape this place soon, and then I'm going to pin you down and . . ."

"And what?" Damn my voice for shaking. It was fury, not lust.

Okay, a bit of lust.

A lot of lust.

"And show you what we've been missing out on over the past six yaros."

CHAPTER EIGHT
SHAEDE

If Charlie thought I'd cower in a cave while she sauntered up to the surface and interacted with the guards, she needed to reevaluate that opinion.

She moved quickly through the tunnel, and by the time I'd emerged, my back scraped by the rough stone overhead and my knees a wreck, Charlie was halfway up the long slope leading to the top. She skipped along as if she had no cares in the world.

I wanted to tell her in no uncertain terms that she had to go slower to accommodate my bound ankles. No, she must wait for me to get ahead of her so I could defend her from any and all threats. But bellowing stuff like that with Vessars around didn't feel like a great idea. Chastising her wasn't getting me anywhere and telling her I was in control of her, and this situation, might land me a well-deserved smack.

Nope, I'd lost control the minue I opened her cell door.

"Charlie," I hissed, grateful her nickname was something used by a male. She was wise to cover her hair and body, and I wasn't doing anything to give her away. "Wait."

She shot me a glance that told me she heard me but had no intention of obeying. That sent fury clawing through my veins. In an odd twist, my cock jerked upward.

"Not the time, buddy," I snarled. "Down."

It, of course, liked me chasing Charlie. It also liked the lust-filled irritation snaking across my bones.

My pent-up feelings made me want to grab her, pin her to the wall, and show her I was in charge of whatever happened next.

She wasn't the eighteen-yaro-old I remembered, and I wouldn't trade that sweet, innocent younger sister of my best friend for this female who sparked my soul like no other.

By the time I'd reached the top of the slope, she'd already stepped out into the sunshine. I took a secunda to compose myself—no, to compose my damn cock— before exiting the cave entrance.

I found her on the ground level, standing beside a cluster of bushes with the head guard. She watched him closely. He grinned.

She held out a few scrapings of brugeer on her palm, and he looked around before passing her a sack and a flask. That was one way to make sure you didn't starve or become dehydrated.

She opened the bag and peered at the contents.

"Not enough," she snarled as I rounded the last bend in the path.

He grumbled, but she held the brugeer out of his reach. If he wanted it, he could easily take it, but she was savvy. By maintaining control of the interaction, she ensured he'd cooperate. If he didn't, she'd find someone else to trade with and he'd miss out on a share.

He added a second bag, and she nodded.

As he tucked the brugeer inside his shirt and strode along the side of the cliff, moving into an area with no one else around, she peered in my direction. With a shrug, she trotted over to the shade of one of the few trees still hosting leaves, where she sunk down onto the ground.

While the head guard was off getting happy, I stomped over to stand in front of her. I wasn't sure why I was so peeved. All right, I knew why. When she was eighteen, she was cute, highly appealing, but tame enough I could dismiss her.

This Charlie kept me guessing, and as an interstellar spy, I didn't like not being one step ahead of everyone around me.

She looked up, her hand stilling on the bag of food she'd placed on her lap before she tucked the second bag inside her clothing. I assumed the rodent creature she'd adopted was hanging out inside her shirt as well. "If you're going to stand there, could you move one step to your left?"

I did it without thought. Then I realized that even in this, I deferred to this puny female. "Why?"

She scrunched her face as she looked up at me. "One more step to the left, please."

Following her instruction, I glared. "Why?"

"Because now you're blocking the sun." She slid something out of the bag and into her palm. "Oh, yum. If you're good to me, I'll give you a bite."

My cock surged upward, telling me I should nibble on her, not the food.

"I'm *very* good," I said.

One of her eyebrows lifted. "That's yet to be decided. You talk cocky, but I haven't seen evidence you're good at anything except blocking the sun, which you're now doing admirably well."

A growl ripped from my throat, but I cut it off, refusing to show her how much she irked me. "I showed you the night before last how good I am."

"One kiss?" She huffed and bit into the thick slice of nullen with a layer of biergart fat. My belly groaned. "You call that showing me anything?"

At least she no longer denied it had happened.

"I touched you." My mouth watered. I *would* like a bite, but I'd never beg.

"You call gliding a claw up my side seduction?" Her head tilted, and if humor didn't shine in her eyes, I'd stomp my feet in frustration. Heat flooded my groin. Who cared about my belly? I could eat Charlie every dia of my life.

Life? Hold on there. When had I started thinking of Charlie and forever?

When I kissed her. No, when I stood in a hallway of

the space station, picturing her lying in a prison, weeping. When Matis sent word she'd been kidnapped, rage roared through me. Short of ripping everything around me apart, there was nothing I could do but rescue her right away.

Instead of a weeping female, I found a self-assured, strong woman who was my equal, not my friend's defenseless younger sister.

I craved her like no other, and I wasn't sure what to do about it. My cock had ideas, but none of them would fit on a prison planet.

She pulled another slice of nullen from the bag and held it up to me.

"You eat it," I said. "Keep up your strength."

"Truly, there's more where this came from. I still have two more buckets to bring up from the ground, and with each round, someone's happy to feed me." She nudged it my way. "Take it. Sit with me and eat."

"All right." Bread in hand, I sank to the ground beside her, landing so close our thighs rubbed together. Her shoulder would fit nicely beneath my arm if I put it around her, which I very much wanted to do.

I wanted to wrap myself around her, encase her in my body so no one would be able to harm her. The protective urges burning through me made me pause. My arms stung, and I suspected the pain had nothing to do with crawling through a too-tiny tunnel.

I flipped my arms over; crumbs from the nullen raining down on the ground and gaped at the markings etched into my inner forearms.

"Oh, cool," Charlie said, frowning at the marks. "When did you get tattoos?"

"They're not tattoos."

A frown took over the amazement on her face. "How can they not be tattoos? You didn't have them six yaros ago."

"They're mating marks, Charlie." I stared into her gorgeous eyes, unable to believe what just happened. She . . . *We.* Possessiveness blasted through me, and I gnashed my teeth. I'd rip whoever came near us apart.

I'd kill for her.

"No." Her head shake punctuated the word. "Mating . . .?"

"The mating marks appeared because you offered me food and a place by your side."

She scrambled away from me. "It's bread. A spot of ground in the shade. I didn't offer you a lifetime."

"You're my mate, Charlie. There's no avoiding it. Now that the marks have appeared, all I want to do is claim you."

CHAPTER NINE

CHARLIE

"No choice, huh?" I said, easing around the scruffy tree. "Mating sounds permanent. You acting like this is the worst thing you could imagine kinda negates the thrill."

"I want you. I'll claim you." He said it as if it was a done deal.

Maybe if I put enough distance between us, the markings would fade. "Slow down, there. We were talking about your rather bland kiss and equally bland groping, not full-on mating."

I was going to ignore his comment about claiming me. My body simmered at the thought. Only by mocking his kiss and touch could I keep my heart from succumbing all over again.

"You *are* my mate," he said calmly, lifting his bound hands to take a big bite of his nullen. "At the appropriate time, I will claim you. Fuck you."

I scowled. "Jeez. What a way to warm a girl up."

"When I choose to warm you, you'll burst into flames."

"You're too damn cocky."

He shrugged. "You want me, and now I am yours." His gaze drifted down my body in a predatory way that should raise my hackles. Instead, I went all limpid inside. I was eager to strip off my clothing and his, then climb into his lap and spread myself around him.

"That's not how you ask a girl out," I sputtered. "And I haven't agreed to be yours or to fuck you."

"You will," he said simply, chewing the bite. His lips quirked up on one side and I wanted to smack him for being so appealing. If he was boring or insipid, I could more easily reject him. But no, he had to be gorgeous and somewhat charming.

"No fucking. No claiming." Even to me, my words sounded weak.

I flipped my arms over, sagging when I found unmarred skin. I held them up. "See? No mating marks. I'm not yours, and you're not fucking me."

He just chuckled and took another bite, eating quickly. "You think you can resist me, but I haven't even begun to seduce you yet, sweetheart."

I gnashed my teeth. To make him think I didn't care what he said, I casually lifted the flask and uncapped it, taking a long drink of water.

I held it out to him after I'd swallowed.

"There you go again," he said.

"What does that mean?"

"You're now offering me water."

"I'm not offering you anything." Recapping it, I tossed it on the ground beside him.

He lifted it and shifted it in the air. "Offered and accepted, sweetheart."

"You make this sound like a game."

His mood sobered. "I'm not playing, Charlie. You're mine, and I'm going to make sure your heart and body know it."

Under ordinary circumstances, my heart would flip around at his words. Okay, my heart *was* flipping around right now, but that was because I was . . . nervous? Nope. My bones were turning to jelly, and my stupid pussy was purring, stating she was open to a bunch of patting.

You want him, my stupid conscience said.

The sly voice on my left shoulder snickered. *Might as well claim him while you're at it.*

Now they were teaming up with my pussy.

I wasn't having it. Wasn't having Shaede.

I snapped my teeth at him. "We're going to figure out what's—"

A shadow slithered between us, stealing all the warmth from the air.

I looked up, finding Warden Gruxidon standing over us with a perplexed frown on his lizard face.

"What goesss on heresss?" he snapped. His intent gaze fell on Shaede. "This is male who entersss prison?"

"I've been here for yaros," Shaede said casually.

From the way the warden huffed, I guessed he must believe Shaede. I doubted he kept track of all the prisoners.

The warden looked from the rest of the nullen in Shaede's hands to the flask and then to me. "Thisss not prick-nic!"

The head guard stumbled from the bushes, wiping a silly grin off his face.

When the warden saw him, his gaze traveled to the bucket of brugeer I'd placed in the secure location near a skimmer, then back to the guard. He raced over to the head guard and lifted him off his feet with one meaty fist. He shook the guard so hard, the guy's feet rattled in the air.

One slash of the warden's claws, and the guard's head lolled.

I gulped as the warden tossed the guard to the ground and dropped to all four legs. He galloped toward us, his claws digging up the scraggly soil. With a roar, he straightened, snatching my arm and hauling me to my feet.

I scrambled to keep my footing and yanked my wrist from his grasp, backing around the stubbly tree.

Rosie clawed her way up the inside of my shirt and leaped to the ground, scurrying into the bushes behind me.

Leaping to his feet, a growl ripped from Shaede's throat. The marks on his arms flared before settling to a black deeper and richer than night.

He tipped his head back and bellowed before flinging himself at the warden.

CHAPTER TEN
SHAEDE

Fury blasted through me. This male had touched my mate, and now I would kill him.

The warden jumped forward to grapple with me.

Bound, it was a challenge to fight. Let's face it, I couldn't kick with my ankles tied, and punching required both fists moving at the same time.

In no time, I fumed, pinned to the ground by his heavier body.

"Should killsss you," he snarled, his crusty breath wafting across my face.

I spit into his face, but his grin only widened as the liquid trickled down his long snout.

"You likesss prick-nic with thisss prisoner?" Rising, he hauled me to my feet, holding me at arm's length. "Guardsss. Attend me!"

Guards melted out of the surrounding area, and I could tell they were all high by their smiles and the way they staggered. They joined us, staring from the warden to me.

"Yousss take brugeer!" the warden's glare took in Charlie who'd hurried over to stand beside me. She leaned against my arm, and more than anything, I wanted to surround her with my body. Protect her.

Flames roared through me again. My body demanded I challenge any who would harm her. I'd kill them, then claim her as my own in the primal way my species had for ages.

"Bindsss them," the warden snapped, releasing me.

The guards rushed to us, and I tried to fight them off, but I was nearly useless with my ankles and wrists tightly tied together. When they released the bindings to my wrists, I snarled and started smacking lizards. Satisfaction was a living beast inside me, demanding I rip heads off and toss them aside.

It took six guards to pin me to the ground.

They tossed Charlie down beside me, and her grunt when she hit made me see red. I bellowed and thrashed while they attached a new binding to my left wrist.

A click, and they'd secured the other end to Charlie.

"Now you worksss," the warden said, spinning. He stomped over to the bucket of brugeer and lifted it into the skimmer, climbing in after. "More," he bellowed from inside.

Guards dragged us to our feet and hauled us over to the pile of buckets.

"Fillsss three," one of the guards said with glee. He shot a mournful glance at the skimmer from which the warden now chortled. Brugeer tainted the air. "Maybesss four."

"I already brought one up. I only need two more," Charlie said softly. "Two." Sidling around, she presented her back to the skimmer and lowered her voice, speaking to the guards. "Two, and I'll make sure all of you get a big share when I bring out the first."

The guards shot concerned looks at the skimmer.

"I'll keep it in my pocket," Charlie said. "Get it to you without him seeing."

"Twosss, then," one of the guards said, turning away. "Big chunksss," he hissed over his shoulder.

The other nodded.

"Come on, Shaede," Charlie grumbled, lifting two buckets. She handed one to me and took the other. "When we're inside, we need to talk."

"Fill me in on everything," I whispered. "There's more to this than you trading brugeer for food."

"You noticed that, huh?" she grumbled as we entered the cave and headed down the slope.

A Vessar prisoner slunk out of one of the passages and approached her. I'd seen him around before, but no one approached my mate.

My growl ripped out, but Charlie held up her hand.

"It's okay," she said. "He's a friend." She removed the second pack of food from inside her shirt and gave it to him. "I'll get more."

The Vessar's sharp gaze landed on me, but he didn't speak. With a nod to Charlie, he returned to the tunnel he'd left.

"Pralk will make sure those who can't work have something to eat," she said sadly. "Before I got here, they starved. I'm doing all I can to keep everyone alive."

My heart ached. She should be watching out for herself, but instead, she worried about those around her.

The fuzzy blue rodent scurried down the slope and stopped beside her foot, tapping it with a front claw. She lifted the tiny creature and nuzzled it against her throat.

"I . . ." She shook her head. "I still can't believe what happened out there. He murders so easily. I don't like dealing out death."

"You didn't kill the guard."

"Not directly." Her earnest gaze met mine. "This isn't a game for me, but now the noose is tightening around my throat. I've got to . . ." With a growl, she started down the slope.

Keeping up with her, I lifted our bound hands. "For whatever reason, the warden agrees our fates are entwined."

"I wouldn't exactly put it that way."

"He tied us together, and we'll make the best of it."

"At least he seems to believe you've been a prisoner here for some time."

"I take it he doesn't pay a lot of attention."

"Only to what matters most, which is brugeer." She nodded to our bound wrists. "I'll find a way to unlock us."

"These are made of bitrion. You can't cut them. You can't burn them. And there's no releasing them without the right tools." My grin slipped out. "There's no escaping me now, sweetheart." Despite my enjoyment in watching her squirm, it was hard to hold my grin when fear kept slamming through me.

The warden had tried to hurt her. Everything inside me screamed I needed to get my mate to safety. Claim her.

I'd find a way to do both soon.

Her gaze went from the binding on her right wrist to the one attaching her to my left. "We've got a problem that doesn't involve your libido."

"What's that?"

"How are we going to escape if we're chained together?"

CHAPTER ELEVEN

CHARLIE

"I'll get us out of here," he said, slipping right back into his cocky demeanor. I swear, it was more than skin-deep. "Don't worry about it."

After slamming on the ground, you'd think some of the snot would've been knocked out of him, but no, this male had more self-confidence than a pack of wooferines with prey pinned to the back wall.

Rather than start yet another squabbling match, however, I just rolled my eyes.

"What?" he asked, frowning. "You're getting that look again."

"What look is that?" I asked. I kept my pace slow enough for him since his ankles remained bound. My bucket banged on my leg.

"The look where I get the idea you want to snarl at me." His lips curled before smoothing. "You know, that's not the best way to keep your mate happy."

My snarl burst through the restraints I'd put upon it. So much for holding it back. "I'm not your mate."

He held up our linked hands, displaying the markings on his inner left forearm. He had nice muscles I didn't like noticing. "This says otherwise."

"Then divorce me."

"Can't do that, sweetheart. We're bound for life."

Jeez. He had to be kidding. My body hummed at the thought, but my heart and mind were not convinced. He'd hurt me six yaros ago, and I wasn't sure I could hand my heart over to him again.

"What's stopping you from having your way with me," I said, "then ditching me because you've changed your mind again?"

"Won't happen."

I stopped on the slope, waiting for a group of Vessars to stomp past us carrying empty buckets.

Once they'd traveled far enough ahead that they wouldn't overhear, I glared at Shaede. "Why not? What's different this time?"

"Me, you." He tugged me to the side of the slope and pivoted so my back was to the stone wall arching up to meet a rocky ceiling. "We're in a different place in our lives than we were yaros ago. Back then, you were young."

"Not that young." My words gasped out of me, and I dropped my bucket, ignoring the clatter it made as it rolled down the slope. "I knew what I was doing."

His growl rumbled through his chest. "You're saying you were experienced already?"

My face flashed with heat. "No. I was a virgin."

"Was." A tick erupted on his temple, throbbing in tune to his heartrate that, for some inexplicable reason, matched my own. It thundered in my ears and flooded my mind with images of us entwined.

"You didn't expect me to wait for you to change your mind, did you?" Thankfully, I could still control my tongue. My heart? Not so much. My mind was also succumbing to his incredible lure.

"You're right. I'm sorry for getting jealous." He shook his head. "Back then, it would've been wrong for me to take what you offered."

"Now it's okay?"

He shrugged. "It feels different this time."

"So you're making the decision for both of us?"

"You're right. I am." He huffed. "Back then, I kept thinking about what your brother would say and how us being together could mess with our friendship. I worried if things didn't work out, it would ruin what he and I had together."

Irritation swarmed through me, a mess of stinging fleetzers. "*I* make my own decisions about what I do and who I'm with, not my brother."

His gaze shot down before returning to mine. "Again, I'm sorry." He sounded too earnest for me not to believe him.

I grumbled. "Water under the bridge, as they say."

"Not if I hurt you, and I know I did."

"I got over it, over you."

"Did you?" His fingers trailed down my face. He

tucked a stray strand of hair beneath my wig. "I never got over you, Charlie. I didn't want to. Still don't. I thought about you all the time after I left."

"Is that your mate markings speaking right now or you? Be honest." Because, if he was making this up, he'd rip my heart to pieces all over again.

"I wanted you back then, and I want you even more now. We've grown, changed, but our paths curved around and brought us together once more. I don't want to cut away from you again and head in a new direction, not unless you're by my side."

How could I maintain my fear when he talked like that? He couldn't mean it. If he did, he would've sought me out yaros ago, not waited to tell me this when we were thrown back together.

"Don't make me need you," I said, the edge in my voice telling him this was a plea from the heart. My shell was cracking and there didn't seem to be anything I could do about it except sit back and see what happened next.

No, I didn't want to sit back. I wanted to stand and grab the reins of my destiny.

"Crave me," he whispered, his voice lulling me, warming me, like everything that made up this male was coated with fire. "I'm ready to give you everything that's me, Charlie."

CHAPTER TWELVE
SHAEDE

I stepped closer to Charlie, fusing our fingers together in a bond that was stronger than the restraint binding us. Taking her other hand, I did the same, pressing our joined hands against the wall on either side of her head.

I was so much taller than her that I had to scrunch over to reach her face. Nothing was going to stop me from claiming her mouth, however.

Our lips met, and I lost all focus. Only she remained, a lush blade of grass in a barren wasteland.

She moaned and pressed herself against me.

My mate markings flared, and I could feel them coiling and stretching, sucking down the emotions between us and branding me with them for life. There was no—

A clang rang out, and we burst apart, panting with our gazes locked together.

"We shouldn't," she said.

"I'm not ashamed of us, Charlie."

"It's not that." Her finger flicked a strand of her straight black hair.

"It's still not that. We wouldn't be the first to get together, especially in a prison."

"We can't be seen," she growled.

"We already have been." I lifted our bound hands as a reminder. "Why did he pin us together?"

"He was angry, and he knew this would make it hard for us to work in the mine. He's hoping to punish us if we don't fill our buckets." She frowned, looking inward, compressing her lips with her teeth. "We shouldn't talk here."

"I'm not sure there's a safe place on this planet where we could talk."

"We have work to do." Her head tilted to the slope, and she unlocked our hands, stepping out from beneath my arm. After scooping up our buckets, she urged me along the slope. Like before, when we reached the boulder outside to the passage leading to the small cave, she stopped and looked around, listening.

The one good thing about mining quotas is that it discouraged inmates from lingering. I suspected those who didn't fill their buckets would be punished.

Actually, they probably starved. Food was the best motivator in the galaxies.

It didn't take long to determine no one was nearby or watching. Bangs echoed through the cave, a rolling cacophony punctuated by the occasional curse when someone scraped a limb or knuckle.

"All clear," I whispered, and she nodded, dropping the buckets behind the boulder.

This was when I realized I hadn't filled even one bucket with gems. At this rate, I'd be punished at the dia's end. This was my only way to avoid standing out. My sole goal today had been ripping down Charlie's defenses, showing her we were meant to be together.

It infuriated me that I would brush aside her safety so easily, but hearts had a way of asserting themselves and cocks . . . Well, I knew very well where my cock wanted to be inserted.

I wanted Charlie in any way, shape, or form.

This was about more than sex, though I had a feeling that would be amazing. To sink into her and feel her body surround me. To make her moan with pleasure. Life couldn't get any better than that.

But I needed to put those thoughts aside. Like when she was eighteen, this wasn't the right time for us. Our age difference would no longer keep us apart. It shouldn't matter that we were older, but it did.

"I've got to get mining," I said.

"I can help with that." She stooped down at the tunnel, her hand stretched up to meet mine. "I have no idea how we're going to get inside hooked like this."

"I'll extend my arm toward you. You go in first, and I'll find a way to follow."

Her brow scrunched, but she nodded. "Quickly. No one can see where we're going."

I knew what she meant. If anyone else discovered the vein of brugeer, they'd claim it for their own.

And then Charlie would no longer have a way to bribe the guards or gain special privileges.

Worse, the warden would rip her apart.

CHAPTER THIRTEEN

CHARLIE

With considerable effort, we returned to my cave. I waved to a pile of something on the floor.

"Fill your bucket with gems and help me work on this vein of brugeer," I said, hefting a cutting tool.

He frowned and stepped toward the pile. "Why are these just lying here?"

"They were in the way as I mined the brugeer. I left them here in case I needed to fill a bucket or two of gems. They'll keep you from being punished."

He grinned. "Smart." While I preened when I shouldn't, he filled his bucket with one hand, keeping the other stretched out toward me. After, he helped me pick away at the brugeer.

"When we bring up your bucket of gems, we'll tell them we're both mining brugeer for the rest of the day. That should please both the warden and the guards."

"This isn't as easy as it looks," he said, gouging away at the thick band embedded in the wall.

I shook my head. "The deeper we go into the vein, the more compressed it is and the harder it is to extract more than small chunks."

By mid-afternoon, we'd filled a second bucket for me and a first for him, plus brought them to the surface.

The warden watched with glee, gesturing for us to approach him the minue we reached the sunlight. "Yousss a team." Gesturing to our bindings, his chortle ripped out, grating down my spine like claws. "Worksss together always."

"I'm going to have to pee eventually," I said. "It's inhumane to keep us locked together."

I could tell from the frown Shaede shot me he thought I was slipping back into the snarky Charlie, leaving behind the one who'd almost agreed to be his mate. But it wasn't about that.

How could I continue searching the prison if I was attached to him?

"Peesss with him," the warden said, turning away to study the full buckets. "Two yousss," he tapped my arm, "one for himsss. More. Three for himsss."

"On it," Shaede said, tugging me toward the pile of buckets. We collected some and went inside.

"I'll turn away when you pee unless you want me to watch," he said cheerfully as we walked down the slope.

"How can you joke about something like this?"

"It's joke or complain, I guess. I'd rather look on the cheerful side of things."

"There is no cheerful side when we're incarcerated in a Vessar prison."

He took the bucket from my hand and dropped it beside his own before tugging me closer, using our binding to do it. "If I wasn't in a Vessar prison, I wouldn't be with you, Charlie."

This male knew just the right words to use to melt my resolve.

"You know what I mean." My world was tumbling down a hill, and I couldn't seem to stop it. I'd either crash at the bottom or . . .

He'd save me. That was why he'd come here. I didn't like the idea that I needed to be rescued, but I had to admit that knowing someone was here to watch my back had made it stop twitching. I had Pralk, but he was just one male among many who'd gladly stomp over me to get ahead.

"I do know what you mean, sweetheart." This time, the endearment came out as that and not a sarcastic nickname. I liked it when he used it. It felt comfy and sexy, which was a silly thought when connected with a burly interstellar spy, but it fit.

"Let's fill our buckets before it gets dark. Things come out at night, and it's much better to view them from a skimmer flying above them than from the ground where you're hunted." Goosebumps flashed across my skin.

"You're right."

Inside the cave, we worked side-by-side, extracting decent chunks of brugeer and even finding a few clumps of gems we tossed to the side for the future.

The warden would be pleased with our haul.

We brought our filled buckets to the surface and dropped them near the main skimmer.

"Backsss to prison," the new head guard called out, careful not to look my way. Which urge would win, his craving for brugeer, or his determination to hold onto his life?

He glanced at the buckets of brugeer, and greed filled his eyes, telling me he'd soon be making a bargain with me. He'd tell himself he would be more careful than the last leader, but it would be risky. I wasn't sure what I thought about that. Life should be precious, but mine and Shaede's were just as important as the guard's.

Time would make the decision for me.

We took skimmers back to the prison, this time me and Shaede sitting side-by-side inside one of them. Entering the main building, we joined the other prisoners lining up for dinner.

When I arrived here, the smell of boiled vegetables with a few greasy chunks of what they called meat turned my stomach. Now, I couldn't wait to dig into what they offered. Hunger was the best seasoning, as the ladies who ran the orphanage always said.

Staff handed us bowls, and we sat on the floor to eat, sucking up the broth and using our fingers to fish out the chunks. The notion of washing hands before eating, let alone utensils, had been thrown by the wayside, replaced with a determination to survive by any means possible.

Those who couldn't work in the mines were made to do tasks here inside the prison, like cleaning and serving food. But they were not offered stew with meat, only thin gruel. Hence my trading brugeer for food and giving it to Pralk.

I fed tiny bits to Rosie, and she gobbled them up fast. She hunted at night while I slept, but I had a feeling she was always half-starving.

"I remember meeting you for the first time," Shaede said softly, watching Rosie grab a bite and disappear back inside my shirt.

We sat away from the others, facing each other because of our bound hands.

"The ladies at the orphanage are amazing." Only now could I see that. Growing up, I'd hated that I didn't have a "real" home, that I had to share a room with other girls and that even hand-me-downs never felt like my own.

"How are Aunt Beatrice and Aunt Trialona?" he asked.

Beatrice was human and Trialona was Evarian. Somehow, they'd made a place for us all, combining both worlds and traditions until they'd felt seamless.

"They're doing well. Aging, but don't we all?"

"You always seemed happy there."

"I wasn't at first. I resented growing up there, especially when the little ones were so quickly adopted by eager families." Us leggy, older kids—those more than three or so yaros old—watched with growing resignation, knowing we'd remain at the orphanage until we aged out of the system.

"It was tough."

"It was a home of sorts, the only one I remember." Aunt Beatrice and Trialona would never boot us out; we could live there as long as we needed. But an orphanage wasn't a mom kissing you goodnight or a dad telling you a story.

I don't know what I would've done without my brother, Matis, and he wasn't even human. His ogre-like species had been caught up in the human-Evarian war, and he'd lost all his family in a raid. Someone made sure he reached the orphanage where kids of all races grew up together.

About the time a truce was formed, Matis joined the military, quickly qualifying for Interstellar Interpol training. He met Shaede there, and though Shaede wasn't Evarian, they'd become great friends. Shaede came home with my brother for the holidays each year, and that's where I met him. We got to know each other better while singing carols or teasing each other at the meal table. Me teasing, the only way I could think of to show him I liked him.

"Your brother told me you were dropped off there when you were five," Shaede said. "They found you wandering along a road in the Evarian sector, which was so dangerous for a human."

"They never located my parents."

"And no one came forward to claim you."

I winced, and he linked our fingers, though keeping our hands close to the ground where no one could see.

"I didn't mean you were rejected," he said softly. "But don't you wonder what brought you to that place in time?"

"I don't remember anything before being at the orphanage."

"You grew up, leaving not long after . . ."

"You rejected me." I shot him a smile that told him I was no longer angry about it. A bit of pain still lingered, but he was smoothing out the rough edges.

He winced this time.

"I left after that, following in Matis's footsteps," I said.

"Training, then assignments."

"So many of them."

His head tilted, and he watched my face. "Including this one?"

"You know it didn't start that way."

"But now it is."

I nodded and leaned close to him, though first making sure that no one appeared to be watching or listening. "I'll explain later, but I've created my own assignment here. You want in?"

His gaze narrowed. "If it's dangerous, I don't want you involved."

"Like anything on this prison planet isn't dangerous?"

"You know what I mean."

"I've had the same training as you and my brother. I can handle this myself. You should be honored I'm contemplating including you."

"I'm here to do whatever you need," he said grimly.

"I don't need a bodyguard or someone to save me."

"Too bad, sweetheart," he said. "Because I'm not backing off."

My lips twisted, but I wouldn't argue with him.

I didn't like being physically bound to him because it reduced my options. However, I had no choice. Now that we were pinned together, I had to share what I found. Maybe he'd contribute some helpful input.

All those yaros, when Shaede came to the orphanage to hang out with my brother, he'd watched me, and as I got older, I thought this meant interest. Perhaps it had, though I wished he'd been able to express it then rather than now. I felt like we'd lost six yaros.

I didn't want to lose any more.

"Prepare yourself to be awake tonight," I said.

His lips curled up, and his eyes smoldered. "You giving in and letting me claim you. You won't regret it one secunda."

I rolled my eyes. "You think everything's about sex."

"With you, yes." His cocky huff rang out. "Is that so bad?"

No, but I wasn't yet convinced I was his mate. "You'll have to work harder than you have so far if you hope to convince me those marks on your arms mean anything."

"Be prepared, then, because I know how to fight dirty." His steely gaze met mine. "And I always win."

CHAPTER FOURTEEN

SHAEDE

I was curious to see how they'd handle me, and Charlie being secured together at night. Would the warden separate us?

We didn't see him. The new head guard led us to my cell and after releasing my ankles from the bindings, tossed us both in together. The door banged shut, and the guard stomped back down the hall.

Charlie lifted the little rodent out of her shirt and set the creature on the floor. It looked up at her, chittering before scooting from the cell. It raced down the hall.

"Alone at last," I said.

Charlie scowled at me like she thought I'd pounce on her. Which I supposed I'd love to do.

But I wouldn't. Well, not unless she asked me to.

To control my urges, I started to pace, and Charlie kept up. It was awkward walking while connected, like we were in a tiny park, strolling along hand-in-hand—without our hands touching.

"Enough," she finally said, coming to a halt.

"Is it time for me to claim you?" I asked, teasing. I loved getting a rise out of her. To add to it, I took her hand and tugged her over to the bunk without yanking on her arm and carefully laid down. I scooted until I was squished against the wall and patted the spot beside me. "Join me, sweetheart. I'll warm you up nicely." I kept my voice low to keep anyone else from overhearing.

This female was never a disappointment. She reacted just as I'd expected.

Staring down at me with color flooding her pretty cheeks, she stomped her foot. "I'm not screwing around with you tonight." Scarlet might fill her cheeks, but she kept her voice a bare whisper.

"How about tomorrow night?"

Her sigh ground out. "I've got more important things on my agenda."

"What could be more important than us completing our bond?"

Her head tilted, and she studied my face. "Are you suggesting there's a way out of this mating thing if we don't?" She gestured to the markings on my arms.

"I suppose if we didn't take things far, it would eventually fade."

"You mean if we didn't have sex?"

"Not really. Some people can't have sex. A commitment is all that's needed. Want to commit to me, Charlie?"

"We don't have time for this."

"Frankly, we could be dead by tomorrow." I ditched

the teasing completely. "There's no better time than now." My voice had deepened, and my mood flatlined.

"As soon as this place quiets down, I've got something else I need to do," she said softly. Her gaze was locked on mine, and she switched to the hand language we were all taught at the academy. With her back to the door and no cameras within the cell—I'd checked—we could converse without anyone knowing.

"I need to continue my mission," she signed.

"The one you haven't yet shared with me." I hated setting aside our conversation about mating, but I had a valid point about our potential lifespans if we remained inside the prison. Was mating with Charlie more important than escaping?

That was a tough one, and I was happy I didn't have to come up with an answer.

I patted the bunk beside me again. "Sit and tell me what's going on. I promise not to touch you unless you beg."

"Shaede." The edge of resignation coming through in her voice punched me in the guts harder than the warden had when he pinned me to the ground.

"I'm sorry." I switched back to signing. "You know I love teasing you."

One of her eyebrows lifted. "Is it all teasing?"

"No."

She dropped onto the bunk and lay beside me. "I don't know what to do about all this mating stuff, and I don't have time to think about it right now."

"Explain."

Turning toward me, she made sure I could see her hands. "Something's going on here, and I'm trying to find out what it is. You must've seen the group of prisoners taken someplace else each morning."

"I assumed they broke us up so we wouldn't be stepping all over each other."

"I thought the same thing for a few dias but . . ."

I waited.

"But then I overheard a conversation between the warden and some of the guards. I dismissed it at first, but then I saw something that shouldn't be here."

"Lots of things shouldn't be here."

"What do you know about stripeene?"

"It's one of the newest sources of fuel for powering hydroforce generators." I paused, thinking. "Hard to find, since it only grows under rare conditions."

"In a non-oxygenated environment being one of those conditions."

"Exactly." I wasn't sure where she was going with this. "It's more efficient than any other fuel out there, and whoever finds a large collection of it will be the first septillionaire in the multi-galaxies."

"Whoever controls it could demand whatever they wanted. Kings would bend at the knee."

"It could revolutionize transport throughout the galaxies because it burns cleaner. It costs a fortune to extract, however."

"It's easy to turn into fuel, which makes it highly appealing. All you have to do is compress the chunks into stripeene dust and funnel it into the generators. Though you do need to keep it away from other elements, or it could go boom."

"Yeah, boom. So big a boom, it could destroy a city."

"Or a mountainside."

I frowned. "You think they've found some here and are processing it for fuel?"

She shrugged. "It's just a suspicion." Her gaze remained on the ceiling. "I saw boxes of glowing rocks."

"Lots of substances glow."

"Few glow pink."

"True."

"During the meal hour a few nights after I got here," she said, "I overheard a few prisoners—ones who are regularly given the special assignment in a different mine—whispering. I swore I heard them mention stripeene. This planet's oxygenated, so I dismissed it from my mind. But then I saw those glowing rocks. I asked Pralk about it, but his eyes got all shadowy, and he told me it would be best if I forgot what I'd seen. But you know me. No can do."

"Despite evidence it's not possible, you think stripeene is being mined and processed here?"

It was hard to believe. Who'd do such a thing, not only with prisoners who weren't wearing the proper equipment to mine it, but getting them to haul it out and place it inside skimmers? Whoever would take on such a wild proposition had to be out of their mind.

They could be cycling through the crew. Some would die just from handling the stripeene.

The warden didn't come across as highly clever, but he also didn't come across as stupid.

Unless he didn't know much about stripeene. He could hope to get rich fast, then take off and leave the rest of the Vessars to handle the flack they'd receive if anyone found out. That would be a mafia thing to do, and I suspected the warden could be part of the upper echelon of the group.

"This is why I've been looking around," she said. "I need to confirm or deny my suspicions before escaping the prison."

"You need to leave this to the proper authorities."

"I am the proper authorities." Her lips twisted. "I was randomly caught by the Vessars, but it gave me the chance to find out what's going on here. My boss had already tossed the investigation aside, deeming it a lost cause."

"They'd never send a female on an assignment like this."

"You're really getting on my nerves." She pinched her shirt. "I'm wearing a binding and a wig. No one knows I'm female."

"Both of those could fail and give you away. You know what could happen to a woman inside a prison full of inmates."

"Pralk would protect me."

I grumbled, though I appreciated her having a friend who watched her back. "He'd be eliminated quickly."

"This is what I trained for," she said. "I told you I studied geology. I specialize in this kind of thing and have routinely gone undercover. I'm little. I look like a teenage boy, so most dismiss me."

"Most."

"I've been lucky so far."

"Your luck could run out at any time."

"I have to find out what's going on here. Don't you understand?"

"I do. I just don't like it. I don't want you in danger."

"Shaede." Her voice cracked. "I appreciate your eagerness to protect me, but this is bigger than that. I'm expendable, if it means exposing this planet's secrets."

"Not to me." If only I could wrap my arms around her and hold her close.

"You shouldn't talk like that."

"I mean it, Charlie. Don't you know I'd give my life to protect yours?"

Tears filled her eyes.

She'd shed her irritation, but what had she replaced it with? I hoped with the beginning of caring.

No, not the beginning. She'd liked me in the past.

Could she trust me enough to give me her heart again?

CHAPTER FIFTEEN

CHARLIE

"If stripeene is being mined here," I signed to Shaede, "I need to verify the fact and notify the proper channels."

The lights went out, making it impossible to see each other's hands well enough to communicate. We'd have to speak, but we could keep our voices low.

"This planet is oxygenated," he said softly.

"Maybe not where they're mining."

"If you say you saw it, I believe you."

That deflated my growing irritation.

"We'll head out soon," I said.

"You still haven't told me how you're getting out of the cell."

"Watch."

I only needed to wait a bit longer before we could creep out and do some heavy investigation. I suspected we didn't have much time left, though it was just an instinct on my part.

I'd quit quickly the other nights, feeling like I had time to keep exploring. But the warden was watching me. Did he suspect I was close to discovering his secret?

With the clock ticking, I had to find out what was going on tonight so I could escape tomorrow.

"I assume the warden is making inside deals with pirates," Shaede said softly.

"And I assume Matis suspects this as well."

"Ah."

He understood. Like me, my brother could be a piece of the puzzle making up one section of a greater assignment.

"The warden isn't selling this on the regular market," he whispered by my ear. "If word gets out, it will raise more than one brow ridge."

"He keeps using new prisoners in the other section of the mine, and I haven't been able to discover where the first groups have gone. They've just . . . disappeared." Or died while extracting the volatile stripeene from the ground. Such a horrifying thought.

"He could just be cycling them on to other projects. I've read mining is not the only use they have for prisoners here, and this is one of three facilities in this section of the planet."

"Some work in the fields, while others are sent to clear forests in other parts of the continent."

"Stripeene is highly regulated because of its toxicity. If he's found a source that can form in an oxygenated environment, he's endangering everyone in the vicinity of the prison."

I nodded, though I doubted he could see the gesture in the dark. "I've been sneaking out of my room and searching whenever I dare."

"That was how you got into my cell."

"I pick the locks."

"I assume you have a tool."

I chuckled, though I kept it low. "Doesn't every interstellar spy?"

"It seems I arrived here woefully unprepared."

"You did bring a pack."

"Which was promptly taken from me," he said. "I had weapons in there, you know. A communicator."

It must be tough for him to come here fully armed, prepared to get me out without anyone realizing he was here, only to be captured. "We can get by without guns."

"In your forays, did you happen to find anything we can use in our escape?"

"Not so far, but there are many places I haven't explored yet."

"The compound is huge. It would take many lunar cycles to search it from top to bottom."

Everything had gone quiet, and in no time, we'd be on the prowl. "As soon as I'm sure it's safe to break out of the cell, we'll search where I haven't."

"We."

I tugged on his hand that was secured to mine. "Unless you want me to chop off your arm and go by myself."

"Never," he vowed. "We're in this together. In everything together."

I wasn't sure I was ready for a complete commitment with Shaede.

He'd broken into the prison seemingly all on his own—going rogue—just to save me. How many males would do a thing like that for a woman they hadn't seen in six yaros? This wasn't solely about his friendship with my brother.

"Why did you come here?" I asked quietly.

"To rescue you."

"I mean the real reason."

A scraping sound rang out in the hall, and I froze, gazing past the bars. My eyes had adjusted to the lack of light, and the moons had started to rise, slaking a bit of murky light through the high window.

"I told you I didn't need rescuing," I whispered, distracted.

I didn't relax until a pale zistarn slunk past our cell. It paused to pick at something lying on the stone floor—a seed or something the creature found tasty. Its antennae twitched and its tail stood upright off the back of its spine. Fortunately, they didn't eat meat, meaning Rosie was safe.

"I'm going to rescue you anyway," Shaede said.

"Why?" I turned back to him, admitting that I enjoyed lying on a bed with him, even if it was a hard bunk in a Vessar prison.

He tucked a stray strand of hair back beneath my wig, protecting me like he'd done over the past few dias. "Things were never settled between us."

"I flung myself at you. You turned me down and left. That felt settled to me."

"I told you I didn't want to do it."

"You walked away quite easily from where I was standing." Even now, the memory burned through my belly.

"What if I told you I wasn't walking away again? Ever."

"Because of the new symbols on your arm?"

"Because of you, Charlie. It's always been you." He pulled the pendant out from beneath his shirt. "I haven't taken this off since you gave it to me. It . . . It was the only connection I had to you."

"Then why wait six yaros to come find me?" It felt like a lifetime.

"I needed to prove I was worthy of you." A harsh note came through in his voice.

"You're an interstellar cop." I squirmed on the bunk until he linked our hands together, binding us physically. Palm-to-palm seemed to link us emotionally as well.

Was I all in or still on the fence?

Damn Shaede for stomping back into my well-ordered life and messing with my mind again.

"Back then, I was still a recruit," he said. "You're not the only one who didn't grow up with parents."

"Oh. I'm sorry."

"I wasn't raised in an orphanage with two kind ladies watching over me and a big brother for protection. I looked after myself." He stiffened and watched me.

Did he think I'd reject him for something beyond his control?

"You thought your upbringing made you less worthy?" My heart pinched to think he'd pulled away from me for a reason like that.

"You wouldn't be the first." He held up his hand before I could speak. "I've never seen you as a person who'd reject someone for something beyond their control, but in here," he tapped his chest, "I didn't feel worthy of someone as amazing as you."

"I wish you'd said something back then." All those yaros lost when we could've been together. "You're you, Shaede. You. A decent person. Someone I looked up to from the minue we met." My voice cracked. "And just so you know, there's never been anyone else who could touch the part of me I handed to you."

With our palms still pressed together, I twisted around to climb up over him, bracing my upper body on his chest.

"Can you do something for me?" I leaned close to whisper. Another glance out in the hall showed we were alone. I didn't hear anything but distant snoring.

"What would you like, Charlie?" The fingers of his free hand glided up my side.

"Would you show me what I missed out on six yaros ago?"

CHAPTER SIXTEEN
SHAEDE

There was nothing I'd rather do than make love to Charlie. My mate. My heart. The only female I'd ever craved. But here in a prison?

No, I'd wait. I'd get us out of this trap, and then I'd show her everything I'd stored inside since I left her six yaros ago.

However, my mate had needs and there was no harm in satisfying them tonight.

"Spread your legs around me, sweetheart," I growled. "And undo your pants."

"Undo yours too." She leaned forward and kissed me, and it didn't take any time to lose myself in the wonder of her. She tasted amazing, smelled fantastic, and the heat pouring from her body made my cock stand at attention. It would be so easy to roll her beneath me and bury myself inside her warmth.

Breaking off the kiss, she tugged up my shirt, but I stilled her hands at the top of my pants.

"I won't love you for the first time here, Charlie. Not when we're on a hard bunk inside a prison."

She pouted. "We don't know if we'll be able to escape."

"I'm a determined male. Trust me in this. I'll find us someplace wonderful, and then I'll claim you fully."

"So, no lovin' tonight?"

"Oh, I didn't say anything about no lovin'. Let me show you."

I undid her pants but didn't tug them down, not daring to take that much of a risk. I'd pay attention—as much as I could while Charlie fell apart from my touch—but if she wasn't able to dress quickly enough, she'd be exposed. No way.

I rolled her beneath me and kissed her, stealing the heat from her mouth. I sucked down the feel of her hand on my shoulders. It glided across my chest and beneath my shirt. Such a simple thing; her fingers on my abs, but it nearly made me come undone.

Stripping the bindings from her chest was also not an option. I ached to feel her breasts in my palm and to taste them. *Soon, mate, soon.* My heart whispered this promise.

I tugged her pants down just far enough to reach her. Taste her. While I stroked through her folds, taking care with my claw, I watched the beauty of her pleasure unfold on her face in the shadowy light.

"Get lost in me, love," I whispered. "I'll watch out and protect you. I'll remain on guard, so you don't have to."

"Shaede," she breathed as she lifted her hips to meet

my hand. "I . . . It feels good. I do want to get lost, but . . ." She shook her head, partly dislodging her wig.

I craved to see her glorious hair once more. Soon, I promised myself. We'd get to safety, and I'd unwrap this precious female like the closed petals of a breelip flower. Then I'd devour every bit of her, taking her over and over until no one could ever pry us apart.

Mine, my heart cried. Always mine.

I moved down her body, kissing her through her clothing, wishing it was her flesh against my mouth. One dia.

Only my thumbs had claws, which was perfect for my mate. Placing my finger at her opening, I delved within her wet passage, pressing in to the first knuckle while easing my body down enough so I could reach her with my mouth. Through it all, I stayed connected to her, not by the binding, but with my fingers, our palms pressed together.

And I listened, hearing nothing but soft snores from our fellow inmates.

When I pushed two fingers deep inside her, she gasped. And she moaned when I sucked her clit into my mouth.

"I have to be quiet," she whispered. "But that feels so good, Shaede. Don't stop. Never stop."

I won't, mate, I said with my heart. I refused to lift my mouth off her clit until I'd felt her shuddering beneath me.

I glided my fingers in and out of her while flicking my tongue across her clit. She bucked up to meet each of my thrusts, and it would be so easy to shed my clothing and replace my hand with my cock. There was nothing I wanted more. I'd waited yaros for this, never believing it would happen.

It was ironic that I'd finally reconnected with the woman I'd wanted for what felt like forever, only we were locked inside a prison.

Doing this for her made me want to wrap her up and hold her forever. Kiss her until she was a moaning wreck. Then do it all over again just so I could see the joy on her face when she fell apart.

"Shaede," she moaned. "I can't take it. Don't stop."

Never.

I sucked on her clit, swirling my tongue across it, while moving my fingers faster inside her. I drove them deeply, stroking her inner walls with each pass.

Until shudders ripped through her body, and she released a soft cry.

CHAPTER SEVENTEEN

CHARLIE

There was nothing like an orgasm to make a woman feel complete. Languid. And ready to fall asleep in the other person's arms.

He's perfect for you, my conscience said.

The little voice on my left shoulder just sighed in agreement.

I couldn't fall asleep, however. Our time was running out, and if we didn't solve this riddle and get out of here, the clock would ping, and we'd never escape this trap. And the fact that I was a woman might come out too. I shuddered to think of what might happen after that.

Females weren't the only ones harmed throughout the universe, but I was much smaller than the aliens around me. They'd do what they pleased with me, and even with Pralk jumping to my defense, I wouldn't be able to fight them all off.

I tugged up my pants and fastened them with Shaede's help. As much as I'd love to strip us both and do more, it would be a foolish move on both our parts. Hopefully, we'd live long enough to be together.

No, I was determined we would.

I lay in his arms, listening, but didn't hear anything. To be safe, I waited a little longer.

I'd be glad when I left this place. Working in the mine all day followed by many horus creeping through the prison left little time to sleep. My eyeballs ached, and my throat was tight. If I didn't remain on high alert, I'd make a mistake and it would be my last.

I lay there longer, snuggled against him, our hands still connected. I didn't want to pull apart and leave this bunk. Even uncomfortable, it was relatively safe. Risking myself was one thing, but I didn't want to endanger Shaede. This was why the agency discouraged us from forming attachments with our fellow agents. Siblings like Matis couldn't be avoided, though they were careful not to assign us to the same projects.

But falling in love with someone I worked with was essentially forbidden. They'd make us choose, and a few times in the past, the agents had decided to split rather than leave their jobs.

I was laid off, but with the information I'd potentially bring the Agency, they'd find the funds to offer me a new job, one I'd be eager to take.

I wanted to ask Shaede what he'd do if we escaped this trap and made it to safety. What would I do if he said he'd choose the force over me?

Now wasn't the time to think about something like that, let alone discuss it. Plenty of time for that if—when

—we'd figured out what the warden was up to and escaped.

Finally, I realized what I was doing: staying on the bunk to keep from endangering us both. No matter what, we couldn't remain here, working in the mines during the day and lying together handcuffed at night. The warden would soon see this was no punishment and separate us.

Get going, the voice on my left shoulder said. *Get it over with and escape this hole.*

I slid to the edge of the bunk and dropped my feet over the side. They comically didn't touch, but after a month, I'd become used to it.

"Time?" Shaede whispered.

I stood and turned. There was just enough moonlight now that he could see my hand gestures. "You can either come with me or remain here to get your beauty sleep." Nothing beat returning his tease. Give him a taste of what he loved doling out.

"I'm gorgeous enough already."

There was no lie in that statement.

He held up the arm connected to mine. "And then we have this little issue, unless you have something else hidden on your . . . person that will end our connection."

I didn't want to end our connection, and it wasn't just because he had a magical tongue.

Despite wanting to hold myself back until I was sure I could trust him; my heart had already surrendered. Or maybe it had been sleeping these past six yaros, and he awoke it.

He swung his legs over the side of the bunk and straightened. I moved around him and bunched up the blanket so it looked like we were still lying there. It wouldn't hold up to scrutiny, but the guards never entered cells at night to check.

We approached the cell door and paused, listening.

When I was confident we wouldn't be seen, I pulled the pick from beneath my wig and got to work on the lock. I could almost open it in my sleep, and a click soon followed.

The door creaked open much too loudly.

Bracing myself, I crept out into the hall with Shaede following, holding my hand. This would be a great time to have a weapon, but the guards made sure we turned in all our tools at the end of each day, and other than a plexi eating utensil that snapped with barely any pressure, we had nothing.

We relocked the cell door and kept our steps light. Thankfully, no one roused in the cells on either side as we passed. Working in a mine all day wore a body out and sleep was a wonderful escape.

At the end of the hall, I faced Shaede, signing. "I've searched this level and the one above, plus the fourth and fifth. My plan was to go through the second floor. I avoided it because it's rarely empty of staff."

"Dangerous," he hissed.

"Necessary."

His head jerked in a nod, and I opened the door at the end of the hall. When I first escaped my cell, I found most of the doors unlocked. Locks weren't necessary when no one could escape their cell.

So far, I'd been able to pick my way into the few locks I came across. The warden's office, for example, where I hadn't found anything worth the effort it took to break in.

We climbed the stairs to the second level, not encountering anyone and hearing nothing worrisome.

I cracked the door on the landing and listened before easing it open a fraction to peek through. A long hall stretched away from the door, a mirror image to the cell block below other than offices and miscellaneous rooms lining either side instead of cells. I didn't hear anything to suggest someone was around, but we'd be quick and careful.

"One more thing," I said before I exited the stairwell. A few jiggles with the pick, and the manacle on my wrist popped open.

"Nice trick," he whispered, grinning. He held up his hand. "Don't want to be bound to me any longer, sweetheart?"

"I wasn't sure it would work. I hadn't tried it yet. But it might be easier to sneak around without being tied together." I took his hand and linked our fingers again, leaving his manacle in place. We'd have to resecure the bindings when we returned to the cell.

We left the stairwell and crept out into the hall.

"Last time I snuck out, which was the night before your timely arrival, I searched this room," I signed, then waved to the door on the left, "Warden's office. I didn't look inside any of the others yet."

"These rooms would be too small for a crushing operation, though, right?"

"They're doing something here. I only suspect it involves stripeene, so I've been investigating the areas easiest to access. Started on the top floor and picked away at each level as I had time, though I didn't look into the rest of this one."

He frowned, and I swore a sign popped into view over his head. *Protect my mate NOW!*

Yes, it was dangerous, but who could do it but me? My boss had ended the job. I was brought here. Only I could figure out what was going on and report the information.

Soon, Shaede was going to have to understand that I was able to protect myself. If we were going to work out as a couple, we'd have to be a team, not him leading and me following.

"Where else have you gone?" he half-snarled, breaking the silence.

I kept my voice neutral, but I lifted my brows. "Where I needed to."

"You should . . ." He must've caught onto the fact that I didn't want him telling me what to do. His grunt rang out. "I don't like thinking about you being in danger."

"I avoid it where I can," I signed. "But it comes with the job."

"We need to talk about that, but I know what you're

thinking," he conceded, his lips thinning. "Now isn't the time."

"Exactly."

His talk about us being mates suggested he planned more than a few sessions in a bedroom. If he was thinking long-term, that was going to complicate our future.

What would we do if we weren't interstellar cops? There were plenty of positions for people with our skills. We could talk about it when we reached that point.

We hurried down the hall, using my pick to open the few doors that were locked, but not finding anything unusual inside any of them. Janitor's closet. Break room. A bunkroom for guards that was thankfully empty. The night crew must sleep here during the day. A conference room that looked like it had never been used. And a few storage rooms that yielded nothing but a dried-up mop.

"Where next?" he signed.

I shook my head. "We'll head outside now."

"Outside?"

"We'll explore the three buildings I haven't gone through yet."

"Armed guards on the walls."

"Which is why I haven't searched the buildings built close to the wall." The guards would shoot before asking questions. "We'll need to stay in the shadows."

"How many times have you been outside this building?" he growled.

I rolled my eyes. "Enough to search the buildings closest to this one."

He shook his head, his clenching and releasing hands telling me he was barely resisting the urge to shake me. Maybe not shake me, but I was confident he wanted to wrap me up in some way to protect me from harm.

I could avoid thinking about his urge to keep me safe, but I didn't like how he handled it.

"After watching out for myself for most of my life, I'm not ready to hand my protection over to you just because you've claimed me as your mate," I signed. The sooner he learned that the better.

He stared at me for a long while before nodding. It wasn't a commitment to backing off, but it was close enough for now.

At the end of the hall, we came to the exit. From the few times I'd been outside other than when leaving for the mines, I'd counted three good-sized buildings lining the wall. If any were occupied, it would take more than one night to search them. It was vital we avoid detection. I'd envisioned myself remaining here for eight or ten more dias to complete my search before fleeing.

"Which first?" he signed when we stopped in the shadow of the main building. We'd have to cross an open stretch no matter what direction we took.

"I already searched those." I waved to seven smaller buildings clustered to our right that only took a few steps to reach.

"What's inside?"

"Tools, land vehicles, big boxes of mining equipment. More housing for guards." The staff to support the four long wings of prisoners on two prison levels lived within the compound.

I'd thought of commandeering a skimmer, but they were too closely watched. I'd nearly been caught during my light search of the big open garage where a full pack of Vessars worked on equipment. While it would be worth risking myself to steal one, it would be hard to tell which might work. Even then, I'd have to override the operations system and fly from the shop before a guard used something bigger than a zapper to bring it down.

Nope, when I fled, it would have to be on foot.

Guards strolled along the top of the wall with razor spikes lining each side. They held laser rifles, and they knew how to use them. Not long after I arrived, two prisoners tried to run before they were packed into skimmers to head to the mines. They'd been quickly shot. Their bodies were gone by the time we returned at the end of the mining shift, and only stains remained on the ground where they'd fallen.

"Let's cross to the closest building," he signed.

"On three."

We jerked our heads together, counting down.

Then we dashed out into the open.

CHAPTER EIGHTEEN
SHAEDE

Charlie's suspicions had caught my interest. I was eager to rip this compound apart to find out what was going on.

But I wanted to hide Charlie away while I did it.

Suggesting she return to the cell could result in me losing my head. Not really, but the verbal equivalent, delivered courtesy of my mate. She had a creative way of showing me how I'd irritated her.

All I could do was protect her while we completed this mission together.

Charlie tilted her head to her left and slithered along the wall, remaining in the shadows of one of the buildings she'd already searched. I followed, pretty much looming over her. I'd been in tight situations more times than I could count, and most of the time as part of a team, but I'd never been in a dangerous situation with someone I . . .

Loved. I could admit it.

I love Matis like a brother, but it was totally different with Charlie. She was the part of me I'd been searching for, though I never realized it was missing. With her in my life, I didn't need anything or anyone else.

This was a problem because we weren't even close to escaping this trap. Vessars were known for being conniving. They ran a tight mafia organization on Earth and their young matured within ten yaros, so their population was growing fast. They were all networked together.

They'd soon overrun the galaxies, which would only become a problem if they chose not to cooperate with the rest of us.

Per Charlie, agency management was convinced the Vessars were running something illegal here, and we needed to discover what it was, then give the information to the higher-ups who'd put together a plan for how to deal with it. It would be out of our hands after that.

My goal was to find the intel quickly and get out of here before the Vessars put even a scratch on Charlie's body.

"Long stretch ahead," Charlie signed. "Should we come up with a distraction for the guards or hope we're not seen?"

The problem with a distraction, as she well knew, was that they would either dismiss what they'd heard if they didn't find anything, or they'd keep looking. So far, there didn't appear to be guards patrolling the ground level of the compound. I assumed this was because the prisoners were locked up for the night and those who tried to break away during the few times they were out of their cells were quickly killed. They didn't expect anyone but themselves to be moving around on this level.

Which could be used to our advantage.

Since they hadn't insisted—yet—that I don a prison outfit, I was dressed in clothing that would withstand most weather and blend in with the surroundings. Charlie wore the standard human version of their prison uniform in bright yellow. She'd stand out like a sunbeam in the darkest cavern.

Undoing my shirt, I tugged it off. When night fell on this part of the planet, the temperature dropped, but I'd rather be cold than see Charlie exposed.

"Put this on," I signed.

She didn't argue, but I'd seen how smart she was from the minue I met her. At sixteen, she could outdo most of us in math and science. Matis told me she'd graduated at the top of her interstellar class. She'd also been fun and sweet. I would've been stupid not to note she was gorgeous, but at my older age, there was no way I would've made a move toward her in anything but a brotherly manner.

Coming to the orphanage only a few times a year allowed me to see the changes in her with each of my visits, but it was during the holidays, when she'd just turned eighteen, that I realized I was in trouble.

I'd avoided her, not only because I refused to approach my friend's younger sister, but because she was sweet and innocent. Too perfect for someone like me.

The age difference remained, but now we felt more

balanced. She'd had time to experience life as she should, and I'd had time to accept that I couldn't change my past. I could only move forward and guide it in a direction that made me a better person.

Finally, it was the right time for us.

I helped her secure my shirt and grimaced, not liking how her yellow pants still stuck out, but my shirt only came to her mid-thigh. Short of cutting off her pants, which I couldn't do, there was no other way to hide her legs.

Except . . . I reached for my waistband.

"Don't even think about taking off your pants," she signed. "You're not running around naked."

"Maybe I wear boxers." Human males did.

I did not.

"It doesn't matter." A shiver ripped through her. "It's cold and you're not running around without any clothing. Besides, your skin is blue. That makes you a target."

Less a target than her with yellow legs, but she was right.

I grumbled but gave in.

"No distractions," I signaled. "We wait for the right chance, then run." I waved to the building closest. "Did you search that one yet?"

She placed her palm against the wall behind her. "Nothing past this cluster of three."

We watched the guards, and when one on the left side of the wall was turning to stroll back, and two others on our right stopped to talk, we raced across the open area and plastered ourselves against the wall of the building.

I girded myself for calls and shots. Lights to blaze in this area. I wasn't sure what I'd do if we were caught, but I'd do all I could to ensure Charlie got away.

The compound remained silent other than our low breathing and the rapid pulse in my ears.

Charlie moved along the wall until she reached the door, carefully twisting the handle. The jerk of her head told me it was unlocked. She pressed her ear against the panel and eventually shrugged.

When she cracked it open, voices echoed inside.

With a gulp, she eased it shut and fled along the side of the building. I followed her around the corner, and we pressed ourselves into the area between the wall and the building that was built into the stone surface.

The voices grew louder as we hovered in the scant shadows.

"My pants," Charlie signed. "They'll give us away."

My blue skin too.

Taking her hand, I tugged her along the wall, racing toward the next building. I spied a door facing us and, without pausing to see if anyone was inside, I opened it and dragged her into the interior.

We stood in the darkness, breathing hard.

I couldn't see a damn thing, and my vision was better than most. Signing wasn't an option, and I didn't dare speak. I also didn't dare turn on a light.

Stretching my leg out to the left, I slowly moved us

along the wall inside what I sensed was a big room. At least the Vessars outside hadn't appeared to see us yet.

My eyes gradually adjusted, and I took in an open warehouse full of farming equipment. There were no Vessars in sight, and I didn't hear any movement that might indicate some were here but not within eyesight. I peered around, hoping to find a place to hide, but other than ducking down behind a piece of equipment, we were out of luck. And if someone entered and strolled through the room, the odds were good they'd see us.

We couldn't remain here, but it would do for a few secunda, and we could search it for any clues. It was also good to have a place to catch our breath and plan.

We picked our way through the room, finding nothing of interest, though I noted a hover vehicle that might be worth stealing in a pinch. One of the rear jets appeared to be missing, but it could limp along with only three.

"Nothing," she whispered. "Should we aim for the other side? I see a door."

"Yup."

"I've searched the next building along the wall, and I know where we can hide inside."

"All right."

My heartrate slowed. I tightened my hand on Charlie's as we wove around the rest of the vehicles, aiming for a door. A quick glance up showed no second level, so there would be no hiding in that direction.

A glance around showed no other doors, so I doubted we'd find a basement.

Voices echoed outside, though I didn't hear urgency. They were moving around, but they didn't appear to have discovered we were missing from our cell.

We needed to find a safe spot to wait them out.

Zigzagging through the room, I kept looking over my shoulder. And when we reached the opposite side, and my hand was on the handle to open the door, I started to think we'd be okay. We would find a place to hide in one of the many buildings peppering the huge compound.

Then the panel on the opposite side of the room opened.

CHAPTER NINETEEN

CHARLIE

With Vessars entering the opposite door, there was no time to look outside to make sure we wouldn't be seen.

We tumbled through the doorway, and Shaede shut the door behind us as quietly as possible. Leaning against the outer wall, we listened, but no shouts rang out from inside the equipment warehouse or the surrounding area. Guards continued their patrol on the upper wall is if nothing unusual was happening. We either hadn't been seen or if someone did see us, the dim light made them assume we were Vessars.

We couldn't remain where we were, however, and the next building was quite a distance from this one.

"Watch to the right," I signed. "I'll take the left."

He nodded.

I tipped my head back and studied the guard meandering along the top of the wall.

The good thing? We'd searched one of the remaining

three buildings. The bad thing? We hadn't found any evidence of wrongdoing, which meant we needed to keep looking. I'd already been inside the one ahead, but the last two we needed to explore were just beyond. We could lay low inside the one ahead and wait out the guards. Whatever they were doing would end, and they'd go to bed.

A loud bang echoed behind us, but we couldn't see what was going on. I recognized the sound, however.

"Gate opening," I signed.

"Wonder where someone's going."

"Going or arriving."

Did they leave and arrive during the night? If I was trying to hide something, it would make sense. During the day, prisoners might see, and some would talk. Although, none of those participating in the secret mining operation had said a word so far, either because they feared for their lives, or they enjoyed the rewards they received for their efforts too much to endanger them.

Rumbles erupted from inside the building we sheltered beside. We looked at each other before easing along the side toward the front. Screeching sounds were followed by something shifting, and I peeked around the end to find a big door opening at the front of the building. A skim-tractor chugged out, hovering only a foot or so above the ground. It soared to the right. Vessars stomped out through the opening, following the tractor.

The door shut with a rumbling bang.

I needed to see what they were doing. It could be related to whatever was going on here.

When I met Shaede's gaze, I could tell he had the same thought. He grumbled but nodded.

We returned to the door we'd just fled through and cracked it open. Hearing no movement inside, we slunk into the dark interior and snuck to the back wall, carefully moving to the other side.

A dingy plexi window on the far wall allowed us to watch the front of the compound.

I spied a hover truck sitting between our location and the gate and pointed.

"We can hide behind it if we have to," I signaled.

"For a short time. We need to leave this building. They're using the skim-tractor, but I assume they'll return it when they've finished."

"We'll run if they start in this direction."

He grunted.

I used the sleeve of my shirt—his shirt, actually—to clean a section of the plexi, making it easier to watch what they were doing.

The skim-tractor was nowhere in sight, and the main gate stood open. Vessar guards strode back and forth across the opening, though I doubted anyone would try to flee through the gap. They'd be shot before they reached the wasteland beyond.

Big doors had been opened on the front of one of the buildings I'd yet to search, and the skim-tractor rumbled out, pulling a large container. The two traveled slowly toward the gate, hovering above the ground by only a hand's breadth.

"Heavily loaded," Shaede signed.

"Yeah."

"This could be nothing. They're moving gems, maybe."

"Or whatever else they've got going on. We need to get into that building."

"They may have taken all they'd stored there," he signaled.

"Something may have been left behind."

The tractor tugged the container through the gate and the sound of its engines soon faded.

We waited in silence, and eventually, our patience paid off when the skim-tractor returned through the gate without the container. A pack of Vessars followed, dressed in regular clothing, suggesting they weren't guards. But I couldn't identify them from this distance and through the dingy plexi.

"Do you recognize them?" I asked.

"I . . ." He shook his head. "I don't think so."

"You suggesting you might, though," I said.

"I just can't tell."

"If they're doing something with stripeene, we need to find out and notify the authorities."

"Exactly. I've never trusted Vessars."

"If this was about selling a highly sought-after fuel," I said. "Would they bother to keep it secret?"

"Only if they didn't want someone else moving in to

take over the project. We're talking about a lot of credits, enough to make many Vessars wealthy."

"Or one greedy warden."

The pack stomped over to someone who'd been standing in the shadow of the enormous gate, and the person stepped out into the moonlight to meet them.

Warden Gruxidon.

The others spoke with him, but with their backs facing us, I couldn't see their faces. I didn't know many Vessars outside the prison, however.

It wasn't long before the pack left the compound, striding back out through the open gate.

The warden stood in the front of the compound, peering around.

In the wasteland beyond the gate, a spaceship lifted off, soaring toward the outer atmosphere.

"They must've loaded the container inside," I whispered.

"It's a transport ship, so I'm sure they did."

"I assume the Vessars we couldn't identify went with it."

He shrugged. "I can't imagine willingly crossing the wasteland, though they might have skimmers parked where we can't see."

The skim-tractor chugged toward the building we stood in, and the door on the front started opening.

We dashed along the back wall, aiming for the exit on the opposite side.

CHAPTER TWENTY

SHAEDE

We rushed the door and hugged the outside wall as the skim-tractor started entering the building, waiting for shouts or anything that might indicate we'd been seen.

The skim-tractor shut off, and a grinding sound told me the front door was closing. We'd avoided detection again.

Charlie edged along the side of the building until she was engulfed in shadows, and I followed. We sat side-by-side, waiting. We'd be foolish to move until things had quieted down.

We didn't need to wait long, however. The large gates banged, telling me they shut, and the guards who'd paused to watch the action from the wall started patrolling again.

Soon, nothing but the buzz of insects and the occasional cry of a creature from the wasteland broke through the silent night.

We waited longer, not wishing to risk being caught, before we rose and crept back through the building housing the skim-tractor and other equipment. At the door on the opposite side, we paused, speaking using hand gestures.

"We need to get to the building that housed the container," she said.

"I agree. Wait here, and I'll check it out."

Her lips twisted. "We're both working on this mission, in case you forgot."

"I didn't forget, but there's no reason for you to risk yourself as well. One of us can avoid detection easier than two."

She knew I was right.

"It'll be me, then," she said. "This is my job."

"And I'm your boss, and I would like you to wait here."

"You are not my boss."

She was mostly right. "I outrank you."

Her growl ripped out.

I'd argue with her all night if need be. I wanted her safe. Of course, no place was safe inside the Vessar prison, but she was relatively secure inside this building. Watching her creep across the compound would make my hearts seize.

"Don't pull that rank shit with me," she snarled, using her voice, not her hands. "This is my job. You don't get to do this to me."

I tugged her up in my arms, holding her

"And don't use your larger physical size to browbeat me," she muttered against my chest.

I liked the feel of her lips on me even if she was angrier than a smacked fleetzer, but I got the idea stating that wouldn't go over well.

"You agree only one of us should do this," I said, trying to sound reasonable.

She frowned up at me. "I guess."

"And that it should be the one who can move faster through the shadows."

She grunted.

"And that I'm faster," I said. "Stronger due to my larger size, as you so kindly pointed out."

"I suppose."

"You can hide here better than me because you're smaller," I added.

"If you're not back in ten minue, I'm coming after you." She wiggled for me to put her down, but I tightened my grip.

Cupping her face with one hand, I tilted her chin up, but when I tried to scrunch forward to kiss her, I couldn't reach. I really was much larger than her—everywhere. Which caused me some concern. My cock wasn't any bigger than that of other males of my species, but the last thing I wanted to do was hurt her by shoving something enormous inside her.

We had to talk about where we were going soon, though now wasn't the time.

I wanted to be with her, even if a full physical relationship wasn't possible.

She grabbed my shoulders and lifted herself to meet my mouth, and I was soon lost in her touch and the tiny moans she made as our tongues moved together.

It ended too soon, though I had a feeling kissing her for many horus before breaking apart would end too soon as well.

"I don't like the idea of you endangering yourself," she whispered. "Who will protect you and watch your back?"

I kissed her again, wishing we could make the world around us go away.

"I promise I'll come back to you," I signed. "I need to get to know the female you've grown into since I made such a foolish mistake six yaros ago. I want to plan a future with you and coax you into agreeing to share it with me."

She flashed me a smile. "Ditto."

"I want to make you sigh from my touch, then start over and do it again. Over and over until you admit we aren't separate people, but one."

"You're making my heart hurt, Shaede." Her gaze remained locked on mine. "I'm ready to admit that already."

She said it almost shyly. My chest tightened; I wasn't sure I could take it. Loving often meant losing, and I wasn't sure how I'd go on if something happened to her.

"The job has to come first until we escape this trap," I said. "And we can't do that until we determine what's going on here. I'll gladly risk myself to keep you safe. There's nothing else I can do for you. Don't you see?"

She swallowed. "I get it, because I want to do the same thing for you."

I tightened my arms around her, dreading the minue I'd have to leave her.

"This won't take long," I murmured by her ear. I kissed her cheek, wishing I could lay her down and show her how much she meant to me.

She was the past I'd foolishly left behind, but the promise of a wonderful future if we would live long enough to grasp it.

After I set her down, I took her hand and linked our fingers, marveling again about how tiny she was compared to me. But size didn't always equate with strength, and this female was tough. She'd make it no matter what happened to me.

"Wait for me," I whispered.

"I'm not going anywhere, Shaede. Just get your ass back here fast."

As I backed away from her, the tremble of her lower lip—the only thing that gave her away—made my hearts wrench sideways.

I stroked her face one last time before turning to make my way to the building that had housed the container.

Inside the building where we'd watched the Vessars, I slunk across the back, keeping my movements quiet and quick, but I didn't see or sense anyone inside.

Instead of exiting through the door on the other side, I opted to lift the plexi and climb through after I'd determined no guards watched this area. I landed lightly on the ground close to the wall and scooted to it, plastering my back against it.

Silence reigned in the compound, and the slink of the moons toward the horizon told me dawn would come sooner than we liked. At least two horuses had passed since we left the cell, and I wanted them back. We'd need more time to figure this out.

With careful movements, I edged along the wall, grateful the moons were off to the side and didn't light up this section of the compound.

I reached the building that had held the container without incident, though I didn't relax my guard. Anyone could be lurking in the shadows, waiting to jump me.

Would the guards notice we were gone? The pile of blankets would help, but we had to trust they wouldn't bother to enter the cell.

Like with the building housing the equipment, I opened a window, peering through the plexi first to make sure there was no one inside, then waiting after I'd lifted the panel, listening.

Inside, I peered around, taking in similar containers lined up with their tops open. A hurried look showed me they were all empty.

I climbed over the side of one of them, landing with a dull thud on the metal floor of the unit. On my hands and knees, I felt around, though I didn't locate anything other than a slightly damp surface. If the containers were being used to transport something off planet, whoever received them on the other end would have emptied them and taken time to wash them.

After peering over the edge to make sure I was still alone, I hopped back to the ground floor and walked between each container. I didn't find anything useful, however.

Subtle thumps reached my ears, and I paused. Was the sound coming from overhead? A glance up showed no attic, just like the equipment building. Was there a basement?

I searched the room, finding a door on one side that opened to a stairwell. I crept down, keeping my steps light. At the bottom, I came to another door. Thuds rang out beyond it, the source of the sound I'd heard upstairs.

I opened the door a crack and peered through, finding a room full of manufacturing equipment. No Vessars in sight. They could've gone to bed; the room appeared to be mechanized to keep working whether it was supervised or not.

Taking care, I opened the door wide enough to slip through, closing it behind me. I scooted to the side and ducked down behind a long, low metal container, looking over the top.

No Vessars so far. The rhythmic thud of equipment working threatened to lull me. I was tired but needed to remain on high alert.

When no one appeared, I eased out from behind the container and worked my way around the room.

In the back, I found a container like those on the level above. A panel overhead suggested they filled the large rectangular boxes, then lifted them up to the upper level for easy transport.

But what were they manufacturing here?

I also found an enormous mound of stripeene chunks. Why leave the substance lying around when crushing it would produce valuable fuel?

Unless . . .

I didn't like where my thoughts were taking me, but I needed to look around further to verify my suspicion. I prayed it wasn't.

Leaving the pile, I wove among the machinery, but it was self-contained, and I couldn't see inside to determine what they were making.

At the end of a long row of machines, I got my answer.

They were crushing stripeene, but not to create fuel. Instead, they were combining it with tetradivon, a second highly volatile chemical.

When mixed, the two created an explosive substance that could destroy an entire planet.

CHAPTER TWENTY-ONE

CHARLIE

Someone was coming, creeping along the side of the building, heading in my direction.

My heart flipped, and I rose to my feet as quietly as possible, hefting the metal tool I'd found inside the building.

Just try me. Find out human females are more dangerous than you'll ever imagine.

The person loomed, casting a shadow my way, and I couldn't make out their face. But I didn't see a tail, and the shape of the head was familiar, not that of the Vessars.

I could be flinging myself at a stranger, but my instincts told me I wasn't.

I barreled into him, though his body didn't budge an inch. Shaede scooped me up, lifting me so our mouths could meet in a quick kiss. We didn't dare take long, but his arms around me reassured me he was okay. He was alive, and at this point, that was all that mattered.

I slid down his body until my feet touched the ground, and he linked our hands. He still wore his manacle with mine dangling, but we'd need it, unfortunately. Otherwise, I'd free him and toss it aside.

"You're okay," I breathed, my voice so quiet, even I could barely hear it.

He nodded, grinning.

I wanted to ask if he'd found anything, but right now, just being with him and knowing he was safe was enough. Soon, though, we'd have to keep searching or find our way back to the cell.

Morning would come soon, and if we wanted to keep up our ruse until we could escape, we needed to be locked inside by dawn.

I released his hands. "I was worried."

"Me too."

While he was gone, I'd remained as still as I could, because being caught was not an option. Secundas had turned into what felt like horuses. My palms were sweaty, and my spine kept twitching.

"I missed you, Shaede." I liked him a lot and could easily love him but fearing for his life ripped through any scar tissue left from the wound he'd dealt six yaros before. I found myself exposed.

He stroked my face with his knuckles. "I'm sorry you were worried."

I wasn't sure what I'd do if something horrible happened to him. Yes, I'd finish the job, but how would I go on without him after it was over?

Don't think about that, my conscience said.

Nice that it could provide a boost instead of complaining about my actions like it usually did.

Kill them all if they give him even one scratch, the little voice on my left shoulder added.

I liked that plan.

"Did you find anything?" I asked, and he nodded.

His grim expression met mine. "They're turning stripeene into—"

Shouts rang out from nearby.

I gulped, and my gaze met his. A frantic look around told me we were still hidden in the shadows, but we couldn't remain here long. I took in the open stretch between here and where I knew we could find sanctuary for a little while.

Rosie cheeped and scrambled out from beneath my clothing. She leaped onto the ground and raced toward the prison where she must feel safer. I wanted to call her back, but she was probably right. Inside the prison, she knew where to hide.

"She'll be all right," Shaede whispered.

Biting my lower lip, I nodded.

"We'll have to risk the patrols," I signed. "Aim for that building."

Footsteps echoed above. Someone was running along the top of the wall, heading our way.

Taking Shaede's hand, I bolted across the open area. I didn't stop until I'd reached the door to the next building. Finding it unlocked, like it had been when I'd searched it, I wrenched it open and pulled him inside.

We leaned against the closed panel while calls echoed around us.

Had they seen us? We couldn't wait where we were to find out.

"This way," I hissed, leading him along a narrow platform with a railing encircling a big open room. I wasn't sure what they did in the area in the center that sunk down about eight feet from this level. I'd previously discovered the bottom was covered with sand.

"We're going to the door on the other side?" he asked in a low voice.

"Nope. I discovered something I don't believe any of them know about. Follow me." Along the back, I stopped and lifted a big metal hatch against the back wall, recessed into the stone surrounding the outside of the compound.

"A closet?" he asked.

"That's what I thought at first. Follow me." I dropped to my belly and dragged myself through a small opening in the back, beneath dangling tools and clothing someone might wear to do heavy cleaning. In the back, I lifted a small panel in the floor. I'd only seen it while searching because I stubbed my toe on the lip. It had been stuck down with some sort of adhesive that had degraded over time. The panel blended in well; I doubted anyone knew it existed.

"You'll have to lower yourself inside," I whispered. "I'll go first."

"Where does this go?"

"Come see." If nothing else, I was thorough in my search. I'd doubted the warden was conducting a covert operation below, but I'd still checked it out. Now I was grateful I had.

I lowered my legs inside and used faint grooves in the wall to drop, landing easily on the dirt-floored basement one story below.

As I eased to the side, Shaede joined me, pausing to secure the panel behind him.

He looked around, but it was nearly impossible to see, since no natural light found its way inside. After I found the panel, I came back the next night with a head-lamp I stole from the building housing boxes of tools for the mines.

I clicked on the light I left behind, and its muted glow highlighted what I'd found.

"Wow," Shaede said, stepping toward the big pool taking up the majority of the room. His gaze followed from where water trickled down the outside wall and into the pool, the excess lapping over the front and gliding across crushed stones until it exited through a grate in the ground. Steam drifted across the surface. "Water, here?"

"The source must be deep beneath the wasteland. Most of the wasteland is swampy. I assume the pool was here already, and they built the building over it."

"Why not leave it exposed so they could use it?"

"No idea." I shrugged. "This is where I've been bathing. It seems a shame to let it go to waste."

"I agree."

"I thought we could hang out here for a while, let things die down on the surface. We can creep back to our cell before the sun comes up." Which wouldn't be for a few more horuses.

"Just hang out?"

There was something new and exciting in his voice, and my mouth went dry. I turned to face him, sucking in a sharp breath at the heat I found in his eyes. A secunda ago, we were running from Vessars.

I needed to ask him what he'd found, but all I could focus on was the rising bulge in his pants.

"I want you," I whispered.

"I'm already yours." He took one hesitant step toward me, and I met him more than halfway.

"I think you're overdressed," I said, gliding my finger along the top of his pants. "How about I take this off?"

His lips curled up in the sweetest, most decadent smile. "Do whatever you want, sweetheart."

Oh, I had lots of wants.

A mischievous idea sparked inside me. "Perhaps I should remove my clothing first?"

His brow knit in a cute way. I got the impression no one had given him a little show before. I had nothing to offer him but me, and he behaved as if that was enough. But I could spice this up. Danger surrounded us. I wanted to carve out some time from this trap to give myself in a pretty package with a bow on top.

I was no gorgeous creature, but in the force, we

trained all the time, so my body was wiry and well-defined. At least I had decent boobs.

He leaned back against the wall, and his gaze glided down my body, making it warm up fast. "Yes, take it all off for me."

His cock pressed against his pants, urging me to give him everything inside me, then start all over again.

"What satisfies you most?" I asked, unfastening the shirt I'd borrowed from him and sliding it off. I wore my lethally yellow shirt and pants underneath, and I couldn't wait to peel them away from my skin and show him me.

I tugged the shirt up slowly, shifting my hips while praying I didn't come across like a bug on a hot surface.

My shirt caught on my wig, and I couldn't get it off. Everything tangled together. I wrangled with the mess, my eyes stinging from both the pain of the wig hauling on my scalp and a good dose of mortification.

You'd think I could do a simple strip tease without embarrassing myself.

Thankfully, my conscience and the little voice on my left shoulder remained silent. I didn't need them jumping in to give me advice at a time like this.

"Let me help?" Shaede asked in a calm, kind voice. With infinite care, he untangled my shirt from the wig and helped me tug it over my head.

I tossed the offending garment aside, then hauled off my wig.

My hair fastener had broken in the tussle, and my hair tumbled down my back in what I hoped was a smooth, lovely fall, but was probably a tangled mess. I hadn't been able to wash it for days, and my scalp was sweaty beneath the wig.

He glided his fingers through my hair, taking care with his claws. "This is going to sound superficial and silly, but through all this, I prayed you hadn't chopped off your glorious hair."

"I wanted to many times."

He studied my face. "Why didn't you?"

"I . . ." Because he'd told me once it was pretty, and despite him yanking my heart from my chest and flinging it onto the ground, I remembered. It didn't make sense. "I should've cut it off like I tried to cut off my feelings for you."

"Charlie." His low, husky tone made me realize that keeping my hair wasn't such a bad idea after all. He stroked my face. "I wouldn't have blamed you a bit for cutting it, but I'm glad you didn't."

"So am I." My smile came much easier. "I'm ruining the show I was trying to put on for you."

"Don't let me hold you back." He returned to the wall; his brooding gaze locked on my body like a heady caress.

Feeling free for the first time in I didn't know how long, I undid the thick binding I wore wrapped around my chest, slowly unwinding it before tossing it aside.

He gulped; his gaze focused on my breasts. Seeing the appreciation in his eyes fed my joy, and I wanted more.

I undid the top fastening on my pants, and shimmied

my hips slowly again, my breasts swaying with the movement.

He groaned, and his cock tented the front of his pants.

Knowing there wasn't anything I could do that he wouldn't like made me come undone. I hummed, twirling around slowly as my pants dropped around my ankles, leaving me dressed only in my panties.

I'd carefully washed them when I could, but they were not something anyone would ever call sexy. I shed them like I tossed aside my inhibitions and straightened, letting him see everything I had to offer.

But that wasn't completely true. I was more than just my exterior. A soft squishy part of me needed him to care for the inside part of me too.

This wasn't the time to feel vulnerable or uncertain, however. I wanted to please this guy more than anything, plus show him I was amazing both inside and out.

I strode closer to him, swaying my hips in an exaggerated manner.

His gaze traveled from my breasts to the juncture between my thighs. He'd tasted me there, and I wanted that again, but in the dark, he hadn't been able to see much.

Now I was fully open to him.

I swirled my hips and twisted around to show him my backside, peering coyly over my shoulder. Still humming, I eased forward, spreading my legs just wide enough apart to give him a peek.

His groan rang out, and his fingers coasted across my ass, his thumb claws scraping just enough to make goosebumps pepper my skin. "You're the most beautiful being I've ever seen."

My skin heated, and I must have glowed. I wasn't a person who needed praise. I took pride in how my body did what I asked of it and that I felt good inside.

But it was nice knowing he found my outside appealing.

I peeked back at him while creating slow circles with my hips, spreading them wider. He blinked, and his attention focused on where I was wet for him already. I did this to turn him on, but it was having the same effect on me.

"I want you," he growled, massaging my lower back and butt, his finger stroking closer and closer to where I wanted him to touch. He teased a finger down my crease, his ragged breathing echoing around us. "You're wet, mate. Wet."

I loved it when he called me mate. I'd never enjoyed possessive guys, but there wasn't anything I wanted more than for Shaede to possess me in every way possible.

"Do you like things wet?" I asked, coy. "I've got something really wet for you. Hot too."

His growl ripped through the air. "You are such a tease, and I love it."

A glance back showed his pants spiked forward. Damn, he was big. I assumed so if for no other reason than he was much larger than me overall. But body size didn't always equate with cock size. Say what you want about size not mattering, but I wouldn't turn down what Shaede had to offer.

He lifted me and turned me to face him, his gesture careful but with just enough roughness to make my heat spike higher.

"You are going to come, mate. Now."

"As turned on as I am already, you're going to have to give me something a little bigger than promises if you want to make that happen."

I burned for him between my legs. My breasts felt heavy, and my nipples were on fire. I needed his mouth there. No, I needed it everywhere.

He took in my body, his gaze a heated caress.

I undid the top of his pants, but when I went to spread them wide, to reveal his body to me, he held my hands still.

"I'm not sure about this," he said.

I frowned. "You're saying you don't know if you want to be with me?" My voice cracked but why wouldn't it? He couldn't be rejecting me again.

When I started to turn away, he grabbed my shoulders. "I want you desperately, but I don't want to hurt you."

The ache in my chest eased. "How can you hurt me?"

"I'm big."

"I suspected as much."

"I'll split you in two."

"Damn, I hope so."

His laugh snorted out. "I'm saying I'll rip you apart."

"I'm not fragile, Shaede. And I'm well lubed up."

His frown grew. "It won't fit."

"Why don't you let my body decide before you give up? Besides, if you truly can't get it inside me, we'll find other ways to make each other happy."

The tension riding his shoulders eased. "All right."

I undid his pants, freeing his glorious cock. Thick and very long, it had soft flaps on the tip and down the sides.

I'd never seen anything like it, and I wanted to taste and touch it, feel it deep within me.

But he was right that it was big. Too big?

I was going to find out.

I leaned forward and licked the underside from his heavy balls to the tip. He collapsed back against the wall, his eyes closing, and a hoarse groan ripped from his chest. His muscles tightened and his body flexed.

I sucked as much of him into my mouth as I could.

While moving my mouth on his cock, I stroked his abs and fingered his balls, savoring how they were Shaede-sized, like every other part of him.

I was confident we'd do something tonight, but if nothing else, I'd bring him pleasure.

He wove his fingers into my hair, clutching my skull to hold me in place. He pumped his hips, thrusting almost too much of himself into my mouth. But it felt good to make him happy. No, it aroused me like nothing and no one else ever had.

"Charlie . . ." he growled. "I . . . You can't."

I could and I would.

I moved my mouth up and down his length, stroking

the flaps along the sides with my tongue, sucking all the while.

His hips shifted back and forth, and he held my head steady. "I'm going to . . ."

Let it go, I wanted to say. He tasted like chocolate cupcakes, and I wondered what his seed would feel like when it shot down my throat.

He moved faster, surprising me when the segments on the head of his cock shifted. I couldn't tell with my tongue what was happening, but I sensed he was ready to explode and his cock changing shape was part of the process.

Later, I'd do this with my hands so I could watch.

"Charlie," he groaned as I licked and sucked, swirling my tongue around the petal-like tip of his cock.

Definitely chocolate. Who would've thought?

His body bunched tight, and his growl shattered the surrounding silence. His hot seed shot from the end, hitting the roof of my mouth, and wow. Chocolate cupcakes with frosting were now my favorite dish.

His hips slowed, and he collapsed against the wall, looking down at me as if I was queen of the world.

"You amaze me," he said, stroking my head. "No one has ever done anything like that for me before."

"They should've," I said, licking my lips. "Okay, *they* shouldn't have. But *I* should've. Many times." I sent him a grin.

He lifted me off my feet and carried me over to the edge of the pool where a small stone shelf jutted from the front. He laid me down on my belly and spread my legs.

"I owe you one, mate," he said hoarsely. Dropping down, he eased my thighs further apart. His calloused fingers stroked up and down my legs, each time gliding closer to where I was dripping.

Sucking him off had made my clit throb and my passage ache. Nothing was going to satisfy me but to feel that unusual head of his cock changing when he was buried inside me.

His hot breath skated across my cool flesh. He pressed his face between my thighs and licked me.

I bucked and moaned. There wasn't anything better than his tongue gliding inside me.

He braced my body in place and dipped a finger inside me. When his tongue found my clit, he buried his finger deeper.

A groan roared up my throat.

While his fingers pumped in and out, he sucked my clit into his mouth.

Moans ripped from inside me. It felt good; I was going to come within secunda. I wanted to bury my face in something so I could let my shrieks rip, but there wasn't anything around.

"Come for me, sweetheart," he whispered. "Don't hold anything back. It's all mine."

His fingers dove in farther, all the way to the hilt, while he sucked and stroked me with his tongue.

Hold back? Who'd be able to do something like that with Shaede's mouth between her legs?

Guttural cries erupted from within me as my mind lost all focus. I rode the feeling to the crest, then crashed down the other side.

He was right.

I was his.

Body. Heart. And soul.

CHAPTER TWENTY-TWO
SHAEDE

I couldn't resist. She'd said we could try, so could I do anything but meet her halfway?

I centered myself at her core.

"Yes," she breathed. "I'm yours, Shaede. Take me."

I resisted my urge to plunge myself inside her. We would give this a chance, but I was so much bigger than her, and I refused to hurt her.

While she quivered and pushed back against the head of my cock, I carefully edged forward.

"Yes," she moaned.

I pulled back out and eased in farther. Damn, her sheath was wet and hot. And incredibly tight. It was all I could do not to come. The duastorns on the head of my cock tightened, hardening the tip. When I came, they'd open to reveal my inner head. That would swell and lock inside her.

Holding her hips steady, I pushed forward harder, burying about half my cock inside her. She was snug, but her body expanded to take what I had to offer. It felt as if I could go deeper, so I pumped, driving myself inward.

She gasped, and I froze.

"What?" I barked, my voice coming out higher than I liked.

"More," she groaned. "Please, more."

My precious mate. She was everything I could ever dream of. The mate markings on my arms burned as lust-haze swirled beneath my skin. It worked its way into my bloodstream. It stiffened my cock even more.

"Damn," she gulped. "Go. Do it!"

Just because she was urging me to plunder deep inside her didn't mean I'd risk hurting her. No, I was going to do this slowly and carefully. I'd watch and listen to her responses, waiting to see if she could handle my cock—even if it killed me to slide into her hot, wet passage as if I was performing delicate surgery.

Easing out, I moved slowly back inside her. My cock was as demanding as my mate, insisting it could handle this, that it could give her more.

This time, I pushed in farther, almost to the hilt. My groan rang out and sweat beaded on my forehead and drizzled down my temples. My muscles shook, and my cock got harder. The duastorns fluttered. Soon they'd open, and I'd spill my seed deep within my mate.

She felt amazing. Tight and welcoming. Her inner walls stroked my cock like her tongue and mouth had not long ago.

Just remembering how she'd given me pleasure made

my body tremble. To think that this strong, gorgeous female wanted me was almost more than I could take.

After pulling my cock all the way out, I shifted my hips toward her, this time pushing in as far as I could go.

She groaned.

I froze once more.

"Talk to me, mate," I growled, barely holding on. My eagerness to claim her fully by riding her fast and hard had almost taken over. If I gave it free rein, there was no telling what I would do to her. I could ruin this for us forever.

"It feels so good. Could you go faster? Please?" Her voice was breathy, and I wished I could see her face. Perhaps I should've taken her with her lying on her back so I could watch her expressions. I'd thought this position would be easier for her.

Her passage felt good. Blazing hot and dripping wet. My cock trembled, and the duastorns shifted. I could feel the hidden head expanding already.

"Shaede," she snarled, waking me from the lull I'd fallen into.

All I could focus on was the feel of her welcoming body. "What?"

"Do it hard. Go faster or I'm going to scramble out from beneath you, knock you to the floor, and ride you myself."

"You are not strong enough to knock me to the floor."

"Shaede . . ." The warning in her voice came through quite clearly.

"You want more," I said, partly in wonder.

"Yes."

"Like this?" I pulled out and plunged back inside, shoving myself as far as I could go. She took all of me, though I couldn't imagine how.

"Yes," she gasped. "But I'm not sure."

"Not sure about what?"

"Do it again so I can give you a better answer."

Denying her meant denying myself. I slid my cock out and pushed it into her harder.

"I still can't tell," she said. "Could you do it a couple more times, and maybe quickly, and then I'll let you know my thoughts?"

My poor mate. Was her passage numb from my plundering? I wasn't sure what to do. I wanted her to enjoy this, but I still feared my cock was too big for her. In fact, I—

"Shaede."

"Yes?" I yipped, sliding back into focus.

"More times so I can decide?"

"Oh, yes, right." Bracing myself over her with one hand, I slid my other beneath her, finding her clit and rolling it while shoving myself inside her.

She moaned, and I paused.

"That hurts," I said, starting to pull out.

"Don't!"

Hold on. I blinked, staring at the water trickling down the wall.

"You are enjoying this?" I said.

"I'm still not sure. Could you go a bit faster and push in harder?" Her voice sounded muffled. It shook, but I sensed she was not in pain. Why did her voice shake?

I wanted to smack my forehead with my palm. What a damn tease she was.

With a growl, I started moving quickly, pulling all the way out before driving myself back inside her.

She groaned and lifted her hips to meet me. Her cute little clit swelled at my touch.

She arched her spine and moved to meet my thrusting body. "I think..."

I didn't want her to think; I wanted her to be a mass of feelings.

So I went faster and rolled her clit, pinching it before rubbing it with the back of a claw.

She panted and writhed beneath me, meeting each of my thrusts. Her gasps joined in with my growls and groans, a cacophony of unfettered lust. No, not lust.

Love.

There would never be anyone for me but this female. She ruled my world and my hearts.

Gripping her hip, I rocked against her over and over, and each of my thrusts was met with her moans. Little tease. I love it. Loved her.

Latching onto her clit, I tugged on it while delving as deep inside her as I could with the head of my cock. I was going to explode soon. Lock within her just as quickly. And nothing and no one could stop me now.

She quivered and thrust back to meet me, releasing guttural groans.

My growls grew furious. I was a feral thing, loving the female I adored above all others.

"Oh, God, go faster," she barked. "You . . . I can't . . ." Her words dissolved into a heady moan.

My duastorns started shifting as seed bubbled inside me. I would explode and even a thunderspry storming through the room couldn't distract me. Nothing existed but my mate and her smooth, wet passage that welcomed my cock like no other.

"Like this?" I growled, diving hard within her. I pushed myself into her, hitting the deepest part of her sheath.

The duastorns started opening, fluttering against her inner walls with each thrust, and the head of my cock emerged. Hot, fiery seed surged up from my balls and down my shaft, but I held it back. I wouldn't release it until she was shuddering around me.

I stroked her clit and teased her nipple, rolling it with the soft pads of my fingers while she bucked and groaned beneath me.

"Yessss." She jutted her hips back, spreading her legs wider. "Shaede. Hold me. Take me. I'm yours."

"Yes, mine," I said. "All mine. This." I thrust my cock deeper. "And this." I tugged on her clit. "And this." I ran a claw gently across her nipple. "All of you. You're mine."

Sweat trickled down my spine, and my muscles bunched. I held myself back, determined to give her everything and then some more.

When she dissolved around me, her inner walls quivering and gushing, my duastorns curled back all the way.

The head of my cock thrust forward, pushing hard against her. It enlarged as my seed shot like hot flames from deep within me.

I bellowed her name, my core bursting. My mating marks blazed and sparkled before calming down to a soft glow.

I collapsed on top of her, completely spent.

Gathering her up, I held her against my body while I stepped into the pool. The head of my cock kept swelling, locking me inside her.

I sat in the water that was strangely warm and held my love.

Her head tipped back, and she smiled up at me, her face filled with bliss, her gaze languid.

"You are a tease," I said, stroking her nipples. Unable to resist, I glided one hand down to touch between her legs. Her body shook again as she succumbed to the last bit of her orgasm.

The head of my cock swelled some more.

"You're big, but you're getting bigger." She whispered. "How is that possible?"

"I am locking within you."

"Like knotting?"

I frowned. "My cock is not twisting around to tie itself in a knot."

Her chuckle rang out. "It's a term used on Earth to explain a cock swelling to lock it in place. I assume your spermies are eagerly swimming." She looked down. "Hey, guys, I hate to disappoint you, but you're not going to find what you seek. I've got an implant."

"You might be surprised at what they can do, mate," I said, sounding cocky even to my own ears.

"Wonder sperm?"

"Yes, they *are* a wonder."

"I imagine all guys think that."

"All guys would be wrong. My . . . spermies are stronger than all others."

"I imagine all guys say that too," she said with a laugh. She twisted around to face me, my cock accommodating the movement, though remaining locked deep within her passage.

Scrunching forward, I claimed her lips like I'd just imprinted myself on her body. Her mouth tasted like the sweetest honig.

She traced her fingers across my chest, pausing to stroke my nipples.

My cock perked up, and my duastorns started moving across the head of my cock, encasing the tip.

Staring up at me, she started moving, lifting her body before plunging back down. She rode me, loved me, and there was nothing sweeter than the expression of bliss on my mate's face while she claimed her pleasure.

CHAPTER TWENTY-THREE

CHARLIE

We remained in the water for a long time. The warmth sunk into my bones, and I dozed in his arms.

Knotting, huh?

I drifted to sleep with a smile on my face and his body surrounding—and filling—mine.

It felt like only a secunda passed before I woke. I stretched and squinted up at Shaede, taking in his relaxed features. He was so sweet when he slept, almost innocent, as if he shed the assertive male I'd come to adore.

For one minue, I wondered what it would be like to carry his child, to hold him or her in my arms. My implant would keep that from happening for now, but one dia, we would no longer be locked in a Vessar prison.

We could have a family and a future together, though we'd have to talk about what that would entail. We'd figure that out once we'd left this place behind.

His mouth twitched, and he started to wake. He was so handsome. So . . .

Wait. It should be too dark in the basement to see.

A glance over my shoulder revealed a slice of light coming through a crack at the top of the wall.

Sunlight.

"Wake up," I cried, scrambling off him. I clambered over the side of the pool, wincing when my bare feet impacted with sharp rocks.

"What . . .?" His gaze was drawn to the light. "Fuck. The sun's come up."

"And we're not in our cell."

We dressed fast. I coiled my hair up and stuffed it beneath my wig, hating that I had to keep wearing it. Soon, we'd flee this place, and I could be myself. Truly let down my hair.

"You didn't tell me what you discovered," I said as I fastened my boots.

Dressed, we hurried over to the opening in the ceiling.

"Tetradivon."

I frowned as I started climbing up out of the basement, and I kept my voice low when I spoke. "When combined with strlpeene, it's explosive."

"They're mixing the two elements," he said grimly.

"Damn. They're creating chemicals to make bombs?"

He boosted me the rest of the way up. "We need to flee the prison and report our findings to the agency. This is too big to handle ourselves."

"Who do you think they're selling it to?"

He shrugged. "To whoever will pay the highest price."

The two substances were strictly controlled for this very reason.

He was right. We had to get out of here as soon as possible.

"I've got a plan," I whispered as I scoped out the main room. We hurried along the platform.

Outside, voices called out. Were we too late?

I stopped beside the door and held out my hand. "Hook us back together."

A snap, and the manacle connected us once more.

I cracked the door and peered out. Inmates streamed from the prison, heading for the skimmers that were always parked inside the gates.

Only a few guards watched. Could we do this?

"Let's join them," I signed to Shaede, and he nodded.

After ensuring no guards were watching, we raced across the open space between the buildings and scooted inside to the one where they kept the equipment. Thankfully, no one appeared to notice us.

We reached the other side quickly and cracked the door open. Prisoners mingled in the open area not far away.

Our gazes locked. My heart thundered, rising into my throat. With a swallow, I darted through the doorway with Shaede following. We joined with the others, only a few frowning at us before shrugging. Survival was on everyone's mind, not the movements of other inmates.

None of the guards spoke; they were too busy chatting together. It was morning. The inmates were sleepy. They wouldn't expect resistance this early.

"Where are theysss?" someone bellowed from inside the main prison building. The warden stomped out into the sunlight. His glare swept the open area before locking on us. He dropped to his four feet and scrambled across the compound, leaping when he got close.

If Shaede hadn't grabbed me and flung us out of the way, the warden would've impaled me with his four-inch claws.

We smacked into the other prisoners, who scattered like roochees in a spotlight.

Hitting the ground knocked the breath from me.

Shaede shielded me with his body as we tumbled. We jumped to our feet, and he tucked me behind him.

I scooted around to stand next to him, determined to face the warden with my chin lifted and a glare in my eyes.

"Yousss were not in yousss cell," the warden screamed. "Where were yousss?" His scowl took in both of us and if one of the guards hadn't come over to stand with him, his hand on the warden's forearm, I wasn't sure what would've happened. We wouldn't be the first inmates he shredded after breakfast.

"We *were* in our cell," I said, trying not to sputter. "We slept there all night." My throat closed off with fear. "A guard let us out not long ago, and after we grabbed some food, we came outside with the others."

"Which guardsss?" Spittle flew from the warden's mouth. He gnashed his teeth. Turning to the guard next to him, he glared at the restraining hand on his arm before swiping out.

The guard's head flew in the opposite direction of his body, and the body hit the dirt with a thud.

Turning to us, the warden rose to his full height, looking from one guard to the next. "Who?"

"That one." I pointed to one of the guards I'd given brugeer to in the past. "He released us, and we came outside."

Warden Gruxidon reeled around and stomped to the guard, lifting him off his feet with one hand wrapped around his neck. "Did yousss release them?"

I could smell the guard's panic, a dank, sweaty taint in the air. His feet twitched, and he gulped as he took in the head lying on the ground, the body still gushing blood.

"I . . . I . . ." The guard looked at us. "I don't remember! There are many inmates."

"Not like thisss oness. He isss small. Weak." The warden's glare sliced across me. "Conniving."

I did what I had to do to survive.

"It was him." I dragged my gaze from them, focusing on the skimmers. "Shouldn't we get to work? I found a really thick vein of brugeer yesterday and would like to bring out four buckets today."

The warden's arm lowered, and the guard's feet hit the ground. Released, he scrambled backward, falling to his side. He stared up at the warden with stark fear in his eyes.

"Five bucketsss," the warden said, stomping toward me with his claws lifted. "Five!"

A growl rumbled in Shaede's chest. I tapped his palm, silently begging him not to turn this into a battle. We were so close. We couldn't endanger our mission now.

"All right, five," I said. Did I sound calm? Because I wasn't. My hands shook, and my spine quivered with terror. I couldn't stop myself from looking at the body of the dead guard. The warden valued no life outside his own.

"And yousss . . ." The warden's attention fell on Shaede. "Since you bound, yousss will collect fivesss too."

I tapped Shaede's palm again.

"Of course. Five it is," he said.

I admired how relaxed he sounded.

Warden Gruxidon's fingers flexed at his sides. His gaze swept between us, his glare lingering on me.

I kept my expression neutral. He'd go inside soon, and we'd be taken to the mine where I could put my original plan into place.

The warden frowned and leaned close to me, sniffing the air. Thankfully, we'd slept in the pool. He shouldn't smell any lingering essence of sex.

"I watch," he snarled, whipping his head back. With a huff, he pivoted and stomped toward the main building.

We climbed into the skimmers, but before the hatch

closed, Rosie raced across the yard and leaped inside. She scrambled up my body and dove beneath my shirt.

"It's okay," I whispered to her as she trembled. "I'm so glad you're safe and here. It's going to be all right. Things are going to get better soon."

Damn, I hoped so.

They took us to the mine. Once there, we collected buckets and tools from the guarded cache and started toward the cave opening. Like before, a group of inmates were separated from us, guided around the base of the mountain and out of view.

Stripeene mining. They needed a new batch to mix with tetradivon.

A low hum rang out behind us.

Stopping at the opening of the cave, I turned and peered toward the skimmers. The warden's craft landed, and the hatch opened. He climbed out and peered around, his gaze locking on us.

I slunk back into the shadows beside Shaede, whose arm went around the back of my waist.

That was when I noticed a band of my auburn hair dangling from beneath my wig.

It fluttered forward in the breeze, a flag waving in the breeze.

CHAPTER TWENTY-FOUR

SHAEDE

Charlie gasped and slunk behind me. She lifted my arm bound to hers, fretting with something lying along her neck.

A thick strand of her beautiful hair.

Had the warden seen it?

"Get to work," one of the guards called out from below.

"One of these diasss . . ." Pralk said from nearby. His concerned gaze fell on Charlie. "You ssshould get inside. Maybe hidesss." Scratching his neck, he shot a worried look at the warden stomping up the path. "Now."

"Great idea." I urged Charlie down the slope with Pralk and a few of his friends not far behind. They shielded us, blocking the passage, and I appreciated his effort. But I wouldn't ask him to stand between us and the warden for long.

"Stop her," the warden cried from outside. "Capture her!"

Her.

My pulse jumped. He'd discovered she wasn't male.

"Run," I hissed.

"I can't." Her panicked gaze met Pralk's. "I thought we'd have more time. I'm sorry."

"It hasss always been time." He dipped his head forward. "You knowsss we waitsss for yousss."

"Everything is in place?" she asked.

I didn't understand what they were talking about, but I trusted Charlie. She'd explain when she could.

"You knowsss it hasss been in place for sssome time." He nodded to the other lizards clustered around him. "Today isss our day, friendsss."

"All right," Charlie whispered to Pralk. "Go deep and make sure you've got a way out."

His eyes gleamed. "Be brave, be sssafe, and be ssstrong, little . . . brother." He frowned her way.

"Oh, Pralk." She leaped forward and hugged him. "You be safe too."

He grunted and wiggled, but I could tell he enjoyed her affection. "Highsss or lowsss?"

She stepped back, grinning. "Definitely high."

"High it isss, then, friendsss," he hissed, his gravelly voice echoing through the cavern. "High it isss." He and his friends took a passage on our left that sloped upward.

She lifted the rodent from beneath her shirt. "Rosie, it's a good thing you decided to come mining today."

The rodent—Rosie—cheeped, and Charlie set the creature on the ground. Charlie ducked behind a big boulder with Rosie right behind. This wasn't the way to her cave.

"What's happening?" I whispered, watching the entrance for the warden. He wouldn't be long.

Shouts rang out from outside, and Charlie jumped. Rosie cheeped; her wide gaze focused on my mate.

"It's time," Charlie said, looking up at me. She pulled the pick from beneath her wig and picked the lock, releasing us. "Things are about to heat up real fast, love. Are you ready?"

"Tell me."

She shook her head and turned to the wall. "Follow me."

We crawled through a long passage. The tunnel slowly sloped downward, snaking toward the far right of the cave structure. Those working to excavate the suspected stripeene entered caves on the left.

We emerged into a different cave with a wall made up almost completely of precious gem veins. Straightening, I watched Charlie to see what might come next.

"Where isss ssshe?" the warden howled, his voice echoing down the small passage. "Findsss her. Findsss her!"

My mouth went dry. I had to protect Charlie—my mate. But how? A glance around showed no way out other than the tunnel we'd taken to reach here.

Charlie's headlamp traced along the veins of blue and green jewels, and she sighed. "It almost seems a shame to mess this up, but I have no choice." Her whisper barely reached my ears. She lifted Rosie and snuggled the creature against her throat.

"Care to share what's going on?" I asked.

"Pralk and I have been planning something for a while. He was waiting for my signal."

I owed him for protecting her, and if the chance came up, I'd pay him back tenfold.

"Insss here," one of the guards shouted.

My hearts shuddered. Had they found the tunnel? The scramble of their claws in the stone passage told me they'd be here soon.

I started looking around for a way to escape, but still couldn't find anything.

Charlie lifted a small, worn pouch. "You might want to hold on to something."

Frowning, I braced my palm on the wall and spread my feet far enough apart to handle whatever might be coming.

She pulled a small device from the pouch and lifted it.

"What are you—"

With a feral grin, she compressed a tiny bar.

The world rumbled around us. Rosie yipped and scrambled up Charlie's clothing, diving beneath her shirt to hide.

Dust billowed into the room as the mountain buried the tiny passage we'd just crawled through.

CHAPTER TWENTY-FIVE

CHARLIE

"I love how you work, sweetheart." Shaede coughed, waving his hand to clear the heavy dust hanging in the air.

I could barely see even with both our headlamps set on high.

"Please tell me you didn't just bury us deep within the mountain," he added with a snort.

"About that . . ." I stooped down and dragged a rock to the side opposite of the tunnel we'd crawled through. Not long after I found this cave, I discovered someone had dug a hole in the wall.

"Clever," he said.

I shot him a grin. "Not me, but I was grateful when I found it."

Distant booms rang out, and I smiled with grim satisfaction.

"And that would be . . .?" he asked, staring around.

"Pralks's contribution. If I'm guessing correctly, an unoccupied part of the prison just exploded."

"Unoccupied."

"We're all here, right? It's a shame our cells have been destroyed. Where will they lock us up tonight?"

"You're . . ." He grinned. "I came here to rescue you, imagining horrible things were being done to you." He tugged me into his arms, and it was good to hug him, hold him. "You're resilient. Strong. Amazing."

Leaning back in his arms, I smiled up at him. "I'm glad you finally see it."

"I thought I'd be in control of the situation." Irritation and dismay came through in his voice. "I told myself I was the boss of you, that I was in charge of what we did from the time I arrived. What a fool I've been in so many ways."

I shrugged, determined not to rub the lesson in. He'd realized his mistake, and he'd done a good job making it up to me. If I held onto a grudge, *I'd* be the fool, not him.

"From the minue I saw you lying on the bunk in your cell, I lost control of the situation, of you, and of my hearts," he said. "I'm not used to this. I'm not used to you."

"I'm the same person I always was, Shaede. You just didn't see it." I didn't say it in a chiding manner. "I understand why you refused me. I was young. You didn't want to take advantage of me." A tiny part of me still felt the sting of his rejection but it was fading.

"I'm sorry, but I'd do the same thing again." He swallowed, and I was sure he thought I was going to rip him apart verbally.

"I had to grow up and experience life," I said slowly.

"I should've stayed with you. Then I could've been nearby even if we weren't together."

There were many times when I'd needed a friend. A lover?

My growl slipped out. He was right. I'd been too young to handle the emotions coursing through me now.

"Where does this leave us?" I asked.

"Starting over?" The hope in his voice made my lingering sadness scatter. How could I hold myself back from him when he was all I'd ever wanted?

I wasn't a shy, beaming eighteen-yaro-old any longer. I'd grown into myself, and I liked who I was now, who I'd become without him standing by my side.

"I want that very much, Shaede," I said.

"I didn't come here to claim you as my own. I feel I need to say that." He smacked his head with the heel of his hand. "Not on the surface, that is. But the secunda I saw your name on your brother's missive, my hearts stopped. Even if he'd been able to come after you, I would've shoved myself in front of him. I had to help you."

Aw. I loved that he needed to do this himself. "I'd do the same thing." I tightened my arms around him. We had to leave soon. Pralk would continue the prison side of the plan, but me and Shaede needed to escape the planet and get the information we'd discovered to the interstellar agency. They'd shut down the shady side of this operation, assuming Pralk didn't do so himself.

"Pralk plans on taking over the prison," I said. "They're going to run it as a cooperative. Mining gems and sharing the profits. I don't think he knows about the stripeene."

"I wish him luck. The Vessars will send others to take back the prison, for the gems if not the brugeer and stripeene."

"They don't know Pralk and his friends. They're tough." I suspected Pralk was royal, though probably not in direct line for the Vessar throne. He hadn't confirmed that to me despite my attempts to wheedle the information from him, but that was what the rumor mill said. He once said he could pull in reinforcements in a pinch. Now was the time.

"We'll send someone to check on them," I said. "Perhaps troops, if the Vessars try to retake control. It would be good to have a friend in this quadrant."

"What's your plan for escaping? Will Pralk play a role in that?"

"Nope." I eased away from him, grinning. "You didn't happen to hide a ship nearby, did you?"

"Unfortunately, no. It's parked on the other side of the wasteland." His head tilted as he focused on my face. "What are you planning, love?"

I loved that he called me that. "Just following through on the plan I put into place originally. You didn't expect me to hang around here, waiting to be saved, did you?"

"I shouldn't have."

"Shaede," I sighed, pretending disappointment. The effect was ruined by my smile. "First up," I lifted my wrist and removed the manacle, "this." A few wiggles with my pin and it opened, dropping to the floor. I did the same with Shaede's, finally freeing us from the warden.

"I enjoyed being handcuffed to you."

I lifted the manacles. "We can play around with them later."

He took them from me and tossed them aside. Backing me against the wall, he secured my wrists with his long fingers over my head. "I picture you handcuffed to my bed, totally at my mercy."

I winked. "If you want your dream to come true, we need to get out of here."

His mouth descended, and he plundered my lips, staking his claim. He stole my breath, my love, then gave it back tenfold.

I wanted to kiss him forever, to show him how much he meant to me. The crush I'd felt at eighteen had deepened to a lasting love. I didn't know where life would take us, but I had a feeling we'd step into it side-by-side.

We pulled apart.

"Lead away," he said.

I dropped to my hands and knees and started scraping dirt away from one section of the floor before looking up. "You keep staring at me like you've never seen me before."

"I *haven't* seen you before. Not this Charlie."

"I'm me; this is who I've always been."

"I see that now." He dropped down beside me and helped pull away the dirt, exposing a metal plate in the floor. "Interesting."

"It was already here, which is even more intriguing. Even better, it will take us to the other side of this big hill, where they rarely post guards."

He frowned. "Someone else used it to escape."

"They tried to." I winced. "I found bones in the passage we're about to crawl through. I don't think they made it out."

His grim gaze met mine.

With the plate shifted to the side, I dropped down about three feet into a tunnel that wasn't any wider than the last.

"Once you join me," I said. "Replace the plate."

"They'll see it."

"It'll take them a while to excavate the original tunnel, assuming they think we're still alive. My hope is they'll believe we were buried and leave us here."

Shouts and scrapes rang out, telling me my hope was not going to be fulfilled. The warden wasn't one to give up once he was angered. He wanted to slice my head off my shoulders.

I pulled Rosie out of my shirt and nudged her into the tunnel. "Go, sweetie. I'm right behind you."

She cheeped and raced into the darkness.

With gritted teeth, I dropped to my hands and knees and started crawling through the narrow passage behind her.

CHAPTER TWENTY-SIX
SHAEDE

I followed Charlie through the tunnel that appeared to have been dug by hand.

I wanted to lead so I could protect her from any threats. But she knew where we were going. I didn't. And the Vessars were after us already. Perhaps I was seen in the stripeene room. I hadn't thought to look for cameras.

If they thought we'd tell others what they were doing, they wouldn't let us go.

After what felt like horuses, I spied light ahead. By then, my palms stung from gouging on loose rocks, and my knees ached from the hard soil.

We came to an opening in the wall and Charlie paused, dropping to sit. Rosie curled up beside her on the ground.

I joined my mate, hunching over while leaning against the curved wall.

She swiped her hair off her face and with a snarl ripped off the wig, stuffing it inside the back of her pants.

"I hate that thing. I sweat underneath it all the time, and no matter how often I wash it, it stinks."

"Throw it away."

She sighed. "We're not in the clear yet. If we're seen, I should wear it."

"They know you're not male."

"But they haven't yet figured out who I am." She tugged on a band of auburn hair. "This is a distinctive color."

"We're getting out of here, Charlie. It won't matter."

She patted the wig. "Still keeping it. When I'm back home, I'll burn it. And let me tell you, I can't wait."

I moved around her and carefully peered through the opening in the wall, finding a narrow ledge with a steep slope beyond. The wasteland stretched away from the bottom of the hill; an expanse of rocky hills interspersed with swamps. Deadly creatures lived in the wet areas, and even the hills didn't provide much protection. There were very few places to hide.

Turning, I dropped down beside Charlie again. "After landing and hiding my ship, I made my way across the wasteland. It took me two night's travel."

"We'll do the same thing, walking during the dark, hoping their skimmer spotlights don't pick us up." She stared down at her fingers twitching in her lap. Lifting Rosie, she snuggled the tiny creature, and I was grateful she'd had a pet for comfort. "Did you encounter many threats when you crossed the wasteland?"

"Too many. I had weapons, though." Weapons that

had been taken from me. How could I protect my mate when I could barely protect myself?

"We don't have much." She sighed. "I've secreted a few items away, however."

"You have weapons?" I asked, incredulous. I doubted the guards would allow one gun or blade to go missing.

She nodded. Edging closer to me, she leaned into my side, Rosie on her lap. "We've got hours before dusk. Let's get some rest. We're going to need it."

While she and her rodent friend slept, I kept watch for a while before drifting off. One nightmare after another chased through my mind. I suddenly awoke as the suns slipped down beyond the horizon, winking out the day and leaving a chilly evening behind.

When Charlie roused, she secured her wig once more. I couldn't wait for the dia when she'd be able to be herself again.

"See that hill?" She pointed. "That's where we need to go first and as fast as possible. They'll be looking for us."

Other than a few scraggly bushes, I didn't see anything on the hill worth noting, and there was no obvious place to hide. I'd only located a few places where I felt comfortable stopping to rest during my crossing. It would be the same on the way back. I had so much to lose.

"Ready?" she whispered, and I nodded.

She placed Rosie inside her shirt. "You'll be safer here, little one."

I followed Charlie, rising to a low crouch on the ledge outside. I remained hunched over as we worked our way to the right.

Turning, Charlie she eased herself over the edge and started down the steep slope with me covering the back trail.

Stones skittered ahead of us, the only sound breaking the stillness of the falling night. Soon, beasts would hunt. We had to make sure we didn't become their prey.

I grabbed a decent-sized rock as I made my way down. It wasn't much, but my fierce protective instincts would drive me. I'd bash in the skull of anyone who came near.

Night birds cried out when we reached the base of the hill and started across the soft, boggy soil making up this part of the planet.

We raced across the soft soil, our shoes digging in. There was no water here; we'd find more than we liked of that during our trek.

At the top of the hill, she dropped to her knees and with ragged breathing, shifted aside a large rock. Beneath, she excavated a small hole and tugged out a bag made of coarse material.

"Good, it's still here," she whispered, placing it on her lap. "I wasn't sure creatures wouldn't get into it. I've got a bit of food, plus this."

Light from the rising slip of a moon glinted on a metal eating implement.

"It belonged to a guard," she said. "It's not much, but

it's better than nothing. I carefully hid three packs of supplies in this area. Let's grab them and start across the wasteland." Her gaze sliced into the night, away from the hillside we'd just slid down. "Where did you hide your ship?"

I pointed to our right. "In the forest on the opposite side of the wasteland. We'll have to cross swamps, then a sandy area before we come to the woods."

"We'll aim for that direction." Rising, she patted Rosie still hiding inside her shirt. "Stay with me, little one." She scooted down the hill, toward the main section of the wasteland, stopping at the base to move a second rock and grab more supplies. She handed me an eating knife from this cache, plus a small packet of food that I tucked inside my shirt.

At the third cache, she pulled out a laser pistol. "Sadly, there's only one charge left." After staring at it for one secunda, she held it up to me. "You were always the better shot."

"Maybe you're the better shot now."

She shrugged. "If you think so, I'll keep it. Otherwise, it's yours. Make that one shot count."

I nodded, hoping the clouds skating across the moons would dissipate so we could communicate with hand gestures. Sound carried at night.

Straightening, she brushed off her pants. "Not sure why I bother, but I guess there's no harm in looking good." Her snort rang out. "It's going to be a long couple of nights."

I took her hand and tugged her near for a quick kiss. "Stay close, but if things start going bad, I want you to promise you'll run. Leave me to hold whatever's attacking us back for as long as I can."

"With one shot?" She growled. "You know I'm not going to leave you. We're a team, Shaede, all right?"

I grumbled.

"I waited six yaros for you to come back into my life, and I'm not going to toss what we've found aside. We live and die together."

It crushed me to think of her being injured, let alone dying. "I want you to run."

"No." She looked up at me. "I won't do it. Live or die together."

If the time came, I'd do all I could to keep her safe. She would not be dying on my watch. But when she gripped my wrist tight, I reluctantly agreed.

Slipping away, she kept hold of my hand. "Let's go."

We hurried down the hill, keeping our steps light. So far, I hadn't seen even a hint of the Vessars, but they must be looking for us.

The long stretch ahead appeared flat, but I'd already learned appearances in the wasteland could be deceiving.

We'd have to separate soon; we'd need both hands free if something happened, but for now, I liked being close to her, even if it was only palm to palm.

She released me and raced ahead.

I kept pace, though taking the rear, glancing around all the time to make sure no one watched.

I'd looked back toward the hill we'd slid down when she cried out.

Turning, I found her gone.

CHAPTER TWENTY-SEVEN

CHARLIE

Oh no, the little voice on my right shoulder cried.

Fight, the left said.

I tumbled feet first into a sinkhole, one of many peppering the wasteland. I'd tried to watch out for them, having heard the passages could fall away for many cleks.

Creatures lived beneath the surface, escaping the heat of the dual suns. Some came out at night to hunt while others waited for prey—like me—to fall into their clutches.

"Charlie," Shaede hissed from above.

Rosie trembled inside my shirt. Poor little one. I had to make sure she got out of this alive too.

I peered up through the small hole I'd made when a section of the surface gave way.

"Shaede," I whispered back. As tempting as it was to shout, to jump and have him pull me back to the surface, I didn't want to draw anyone's attention.

His face poked into the hole. "You're all right?" His gaze slid down my front, assessing for damage.

"So far."

"Grab my hand." He stretched it downward.

I scooted over to stand beneath him, looking for something to stand on. I'd fallen about ten feet, and despite his greater height, he wasn't going to be able to reach me even if I jumped. Spying a small boulder, I hurried to it and started rolling it into the center of the small cave.

He leaned in farther. "I've got you." The surface around him gave way, and he fell, landing squarely on his feet beside me. His scowl took in the larger opening before he peered around, his gaze eventually falling on me. "Let me boost you up."

"I won't be able to pull you up after."

"I can jump."

I nibbled on my lower lip for a minue. "Okay."

He made a sling with his hands, and I stepped onto it, using his shoulders to maintain my balance.

He shot me up through the opening, and I landed on my belly along the outer lip.

Rosie scurried out from beneath my shirt, scrambling up the hill. She turned toward me and whimpered.

The edge beneath me gave way, and I fell back inside, Shaede scooped me from the air before I hit. He lowered me to my feet.

"Should we use the boulders?" I asked. "We need to climb out away from the edge. It keeps crumbling.

Maybe if we're higher to begin with, we can pick a thicker side to climb out on."

He grunted and rolled a large boulder beneath the opening.

I took in the small cave with its rounded, scraped rock surface, spying an oval opening on the side at knee-height. Darkness filled a tunnel. If something was watching us from inside, it wasn't being obvious about it.

About ten feet across, the cave had a damp dirt floor scattered with small rocks and bones. Good sized bones, too, indicating something brought prey here and ate it or creatures fell through the sinkhole like we had but couldn't climb back out.

A shiver tracked through me. I was a tough woman; I never would've made it through my training if I wasn't. But the thought of running into whatever ate prey here made me eager to get back to the surface.

"Climb onto my shoulders," Shaede said from where he was perched on the top of the boulder, gripping the lip of the opening above. "You should be able to scramble out." He tapped the edge. "This is the strongest side."

I wasn't confident he'd be able to get out himself, but we had to start somewhere.

A scraping sound erupted from the dark passage. My pulse surged up into my throat, and my skin crawled. The little voices on my shoulders told me to run.

I climbed Shaede like a tree, soon standing on his shoulders, his big hands wrapped around my ankles to give me stability. The lip of the opening appeared too thin, but the scrapes were growing louder in the tunnel. Something big was coming this way.

I scrambled up onto the thickest part of the surface, hoping it would bear my weight.

It crumbled beneath me, raining down chunks of soil and rock.

"Keep going," he hissed, his gaze shooting to the passage.

Each time I tried, however, more of the surface collapsed. I started hitting it, breaking it off in the hope of reaching where the wall supported the surface from below.

Shaede's sucked in breath made me pause and look down.

A wild, furry beast with eight legs had latched onto his leg, clawing and biting, ripping through his pants.

"Let me down. We have to get it off you."

I dropped fast, and the moment my feet touched the ground, I pulled the eating knife I'd stolen from the guard's dining area. I slashed out, hitting the back of the creature. It whirled, leaping toward me, hitting my chest so hard that I fell on my side.

The wind was knocked from me. I grappled with the creature, gripping its mane while it slathered and tried to rip out my throat.

Shaede grabbed the creature and wrenched it off me, tossing it toward the wall with super-human strength. It hit hard and slumped down on the surface, leaving a bloody streak behind. Thankfully, it didn't move again.

I sat up, panting, and ran my hands across my neck and arms, finding no wounds.

Shaede dropped down to the ground beside me and tugged up his pants, revealing puncture marks from the creature's fangs. They'd stabbed deeply, and blood trickled down his leg.

With my knife, I sliced a strip of the hem from my shirt and wrapped his wounds. "You need an antibiotic zap."

"There's a med kit in my ship."

"Then we need to get there fast."

After pulling his pants down over his leg, he stood and offered me a hand to stand, something that crushed my heart. Here he was, injured, and he still thought of helping me.

I took his hand, though. He wanted to do this, and it made him happy. My life had revolved around showing everyone I was strong, that I could do whatever I needed to all by myself. Independence was a badge I wore on my chest.

But maybe it would be okay to share strength with Shaede. I'd told him we'd live or die together, expecting him to metaphorically step toward me. But when I said it, I hadn't considered I'd need to do the same thing.

Tossing the knife aside, I barreled into him, hugging him, not saying anything but giving him my warmth and strength.

"What was that for?" he asked, patting my back.

"Because you're you." His shirt muffled my voice, and my eyes stung. I couldn't cry; he'd want to fix that too.

There was no fixing this. I needed to feel these emotions for him, this trust. "You're my mate, you know."

His arms tightened around me. "I knew that the minue I saw you lying on that bunk. I'm sorry I hurt you all those yaros ago. If I could make it up to you, I would."

"There's nothing to make up for. We're different people than we were back then. We're together now, and that's all that matters."

He lifted me for a quick kiss, then shot me a grin. "Does this mean you'll let me do whatever I want with you?"

I chuckled. "Sometimes."

His brows shot up. "Only sometimes?"

"Always," I said against his mouth.

"Let's get out of this trap and make our way across the wasteland. My ship has food and a cleansing unit."

"I'd almost kill for a cleansing unit."

"We'll climb inside it together."

CHAPTER TWENTY-EIGHT

SHAEDE

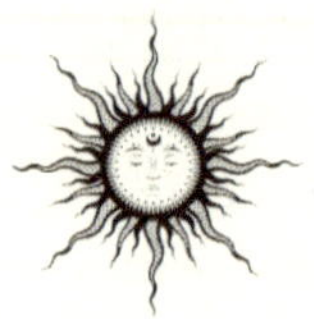

"I was thinking," Charlie said, looking up at the opening. The moons had risen further, shedding enough light that we'd be able to trek through the wasteland more easily.

If we could get back to the surface.

"If we break off the edges until we reach the cave's wall," she said, "it might support us enough to climb out."

I handed her a rock from the floor. "Use this."

"I like that you listen to my idea and that you're willing to give it a try. No arguing that you have to be the one to do it."

"If you could lift me up, sweetheart, I'd do it for you, but that's impossible. And none of the boulders are large enough for me to stand on and still reach."

She sighed. "You were scoring points, Shaede. Scoring big ones. And now you've ruined it."

I chuckled. "You're the best one to do this. I mean that."

"Thanks."

I held her ankles while she slowly worked across the ledge with dirt and bits of rock raining down on me.

"The only bad thing about this is it makes noise," she whispered.

"Not for long."

I kept my eye on the passage, wondering if the creature who'd attacked had friends. So far, I didn't hear anything, but I'd be foolish to ignore the possibility.

"Finally," Charlie said. She dropped the rock down beside me and lifted herself up onto the edge. "Holding so far."

Her legs dangled, scrambling as she worked the rest of her body up onto the top.

I breathed a sigh of relief when she turned and peered down into the hole, holding Rosie in her arms.

"Your turn now," she said, backing away.

I leaped, grabbing the edge, and used the nearby wall to work my way up onto the upper level. With my legs hanging in the hole, I dragged myself along the top until I'd left the cave behind.

On my feet again, I took her hand. "Don't let go."

She nodded, relief shoving aside the shadows in her eyes.

A glance around showed nothing of concern, but we needed to put as much distance between us and the prison as possible. After she put Rosie inside her shirt and the knife into the back waistband of her pants, we took off, moving as fast as we dared. The last thing we wanted to do was fall into a sinkhole again. The next time, we might not get out.

"Here," she whispered, tugging me up another rise covered with scraggly tall grass. "I left a few more things here we might be able to use." At the top of the low hill, she released my hand and carefully shifted aside a mound of rocks, peeling back a layer of grass. She tugged out a bag and stood, securing it to her back. "Simple stuff, but it'll come in handy."

"What is it?"

"Camo tent."

I released a low whistle. "Where did you find that?"

"In a closet inside the warden's office."

"You're amazing." A camo tent could be set up anywhere to provide complete protection from the elements. Like a chameleon, it would mask itself to blend in with the surroundings.

I hoped we wouldn't need it, but we'd spent more time in the cave than I liked.

We ate fast, drinking some of our water, then strode out into the wasteland, holding hands.

"This is going to be the hardest part," she signed. "We'll need to be very quiet."

The creature in the cave was one of the many dangers in this area. I'd fought off beasts multiple times while making my way toward the prison.

A fierce need to protect Charlie rose within me, and I

didn't tamp it down. Stress heightened awareness, and my senses needed to work in high gear.

And that was why I heard the soft pads of something coming toward us from behind.

CHAPTER TWENTY-NINE

CHARLIE

"Run," he hissed, snatching up my hand and bolting.

I raced beside him, unsure what had spooked him, but believing when he said run, he had a solid reason.

Slaps erupted behind us, and I shot a glance over my shoulder. What I saw made fear slam through me. With the knife in my hand, I ran faster, praying the enormous pack of creatures stomping across the wasteland floor didn't catch up.

I'd only heard about willarveeps, and I never thought I'd encounter one here, let alone a pack of them. They were plants that thrived in wet areas and could uproot themselves to move at will. Their tentacled limbs would latch onto your skin and leave a welt, but that wasn't the worst thing they could do. They'd drag you close and suck you down their gaping maws. Their fanged jaws would snap shut, trapping you inside, and the walls of the mouth would secrete an acidic solution to digest you slowly.

"Get ahead of me," Shaede said. "Run and don't look back."

"You plan to," I panted, "fight them off alone?"

"Yes."

"No." Jeez, were we locked in this argument again? When was he going to realize I could defend myself? Sure, I loved his support, but I'd tackled numerous threats without him pushing me to the side.

"Charlie," he warned.

"Shaede. Live or die together, remember? Or am I the only one who truly believes that?"

For one secunda, he looked shocked. Then the realization hit him. He kept running, me keeping up, but resolution had taken over the stunned look on his face.

"You're right," he puffed. "I'm sorry."

"Make it up to me later."

He saluted me and ran faster. I sped along beside him until we reached a wet area.

He'd crossed this section already, so he knew what to expect, but I told him anyway.

"Leap from one small island to the next."

"Will do," he said with a chuckle.

I knew where he was going with his laughter. Maybe I wasn't that much different from him. We were two strong personalities, each trying to take control. Could we find a way to meet in the middle?

We had to release each other's hands to continue, but

I kept an eye on him and by the way he kept glancing in my direction, he did the same.

That was more like it. We could watch out for each other without always being in charge of what the other person was doing.

Snaps and croaks rang out behind us, and when I looked back, I came to a stop, watching in awe as the willarveep's natural predator claimed one plant after another.

"Beasts live in the water," I said, staring down at the murky depths surrounding the small spit of land I stood upon. "I imagine they eat people as eagerly as willarveeps."

He nodded and kept the laser pistol in his hand. We bolted again, aiming for a raised area ahead. The island would give way to more swamp, but we'd be safe from the creatures lurking in the water while on dry land.

Behind us, the beasts snatched up the willarveeps, gobbling them down until there were none left to come after us.

Hopefully, the water creatures' appetites were satisfied, and they wouldn't seek us for dessert.

Thankfully, we had moonlight to guide us. And our headlamps, though we wouldn't use them unless we absolutely had to. They'd draw the Vessars to us, and the Vessars wouldn't need to run through the wasteland. They could shoot at us from the skimmers or swoop down inside other vehicles that could scoop us up and take us back to the prison.

We leaped onto the large island in unison and raced

up the gradual slope, slowing when we reached the broad top to catch our breath.

"The swamp creatures won't follow," he said softly.

"What makes you think that?"

He shrugged. "They didn't climb onto dry land when I encountered them the first time."

Good enough for me.

He turned in a slow circle, taking in the surrounding area. "No more willarveeps, then."

Not yet.

"I haven't traveled the wasteland other than the outer areas and only quickly to bury supplies," I said. "I quizzed everyone I could about what to expect, but I didn't learn much. How much of this part of the planet is made up of swamp?"

"We have horuses of travel still." He studied the area, taking in the scruffy trees barely taller than him and the moons sinking toward the horizon. He flicked the safety on the laser pistol and tucked it into the back of his pants. "It's almost dawn. We should set up your tent near the trees and get some rest. We can finish the journey when the suns go down."

We approached the trees, watching for movement. Dry land might be safer than the water, but that didn't mean there weren't threats here as well. But we found nothing lurking on the ground or among the spindly branches.

It didn't take long to set up the tent. We crawled inside.

Rosie remained outside, flopping down along the

edge of the tent and quickly falling asleep. After she woke, I assumed she'd hunt like she did at night inside the prison.

"Not much room," Shaede said, taking in the tiny space.

"It's made for one person."

"An alien of my size or a tiny human?"

I grinned and started removing my clothing. "I imagine we can make it work, don't you?"

"Definitely mate. Definitely."

In no time, we were naked. We tumbled to the canvas surface, entwined.

I rose above him, watching the heat grow in his eyes.

"You're mine," I said, stroking his face and chest. "Mine." I kept whispering the word as I kissed along his jawline and down his neck. "No one is going to take you away from me."

"Mate," he groaned. "I am happily yours."

"Love me," I said. "I need to feel close to you." Danger surrounded us, and we still had more of the wasteland to cross. What if we didn't survive the night?

I wanted this minue with the male I'd love for eternity.

"I do, mate. I do." He shifted us around until I was beneath him.

He kissed down my throat, his mouth sweet and tender. Sometimes, things didn't need to be rushed. There was something amazing about savoring each secunda rather than hurrying to what waited next. He'd soon claim me and me him, but it was wonderful to enjoy each kiss and touch that brought out my sighs and heightened my pleasure in just being with him.

He was the wine to my soul and the heat in my veins.

I moaned and arched my back, seeking his tender touch. His skin rubbed against mine as he took my nipple into his mouth and ran his tongue across it.

"You're beautiful," he whispered against my breast. "All I could ever desire. My soul would recognize yours no matter who we were and where life takes us. You are mine, but it's so much more than that. This isn't about possessing or controlling you, but about offering myself and taking whatever you're willing to give."

"All of me, Shaede. I give everything I am."

"I want to touch and taste you."

"Take me."

He grinned up at me as he kissed across my belly. "Only if you take me too."

"Yes," I breathed, smiling right back at him.

His fingers teased across my clit, and fire burst inside me, a roaring inferno only he could extinguish.

"You smell amazing," he said. "Like lust and love and the beauty of everything you've brought to my life."

He sucked my clit into his mouth and rolled it while his fingers stroked down my slit.

His fingers slid inside me, pumping, drawing out my gasps with each stroke.

I was wet for him. I loved that he could turn me on so fast.

He spread my thighs wider. "Come for me, mate. Give me your joy so I can give it back tenfold."

"Shaede," I breathed. "Take me now."

"Come," he growled, pushing inside me harder, faster. He sucked on my clit, and all I could focus on was his mouth and fingers. I was lost, and only he could guide me to where I ached to be.

My back arched, and I bucked against him.

"I want this," he said. "Give it to me." He pulled his fingers out, leaving me gasping, and licked them clean. "More." They went back inside me, drawing out my excitement.

He hummed against my clit, driving me higher. The sound coasted through my bones, sinking into me. My chest felt like it would burst wide open with love for him.

"Soar to the stars, love," he whispered before sucking on my clit again. "I'll be right with you."

My body gave way, a dam let loose. Ripples shot through me, and I moaned out his name.

"Shaede," I whispered as my body started to come back to the ground. "You . . ." I wasn't sure what to say. He gave and gave, rarely taking, and that crushed me.

He lifted his head, his fingers still moving slowly inside me.

I'd never been a woman who could have more than one orgasm in an evening, but I could feel it building inside me all over again.

Shaede was the difference. It was never good to compare, but how could anyone take the place of the guy I'd loved almost from the minue I met him? He'd always been the one for me. Knowing he wanted me as much gave me confidence. A certainty that no matter what, we'd be together.

"I want you, mate," he said with such sweet vulnerability.

My heart split wide open again. It ached, but it felt amazing. "Be with me, mate. Be with me always."

He pressed his palm against his chest. "Always."

Rising over me, he centered his cock at my opening. He was big and thick, but we'd already proved he fit. I loved how he stretched me, filled me, and how he made sure I felt pleasure before seeking his own.

I hitched my legs around him, spreading myself to take everything he was about to give.

He pushed forward, stretching me with a subtle sting that only made it feel better. I wanted the blissful escape only he could bring.

Pulling back, he drove forward again, seating himself fully inside me.

His groan rang out in the small space. "You feel wonderful. So tight and wet. I'll never get enough."

Our soft cries echoed in the small tent.

He maintained a slow pace, milking every bit of satisfaction from me. I was spiraling, coiling tight, before releasing all over again. Each movement showed me how deeply he cared, how much I meant to him, and it was beautiful. Tears stung in my eyes.

My orgasm caught up with me much too quickly, a burst of heat shooting through my core.

He moved faster to drive the feeling home before pulling out and turning me onto my belly.

Lifting my hips, he spread me wide. He moved down and licked me. "You taste like love, mate. Me and you." His tongue stroked my clit as ripples continued through me, each one more powerful than the last.

He rose over me and drove inside me again.

I gasped and arched up to meet him, seeking that wonderful feeling once more. My moan ripped from me as he moved faster.

"Yes," I cried. "Shaede."

I felt the flaps on the end of his cock open, flaring within me, and I came once more.

The head of his cock swelled impossibly big as he shoved it deep within me again.

His hot seed shot from him, bathing my inner walls.

Impossibly, I came again, each pleasurable shudder better than the last.

"Mate," he said, shifting his swollen cock within me, though he could barely move it now that it had knotted. "Mate."

He lay on top of me, bracing himself to hold back most of his weight.

I loved the feeling of being surrounded by him, as if nothing and no one could ever harm me as long as I was within his embrace.

Easing onto his side, he took me with him, maintaining our connection.

His fingers glided across my thigh and delved between my legs, finding my swollen clit. He stroked it, lightly teasing it while small quivers wracked my inner passage.

"Love you, mate," he said softly. "Love you so much. You're the home I've sought all my life. My heart. My soul. My reason to keep living."

"Shaede." My eyes stung all over again. Each time I thought I couldn't love him more, he wiggled deeper into my heart. "Love you too."

He continued to gently stroke my clit; his cock locked tight within me.

I wasn't sure how my body could give more, but it did, slowly building back to yet another orgasm.

He claimed it as his own like he'd just claimed everything else I had to give.

CHAPTER THIRTY
SHAEDE

I woke with Charlie in my arms and my cock still buried deep inside her.

She slept, and I held her, grateful she was able to find rest. From the darkness eclipsing the tent, the suns must've set while we slept.

We needed to start walking again, but I was greedy. All I wanted to do was lie here with her for the rest of my dias.

She stirred and came awake all at once, stretching.

"Someone's feeling frisky this morning," she said with a satisfied laugh. "Night. Whatever it might be."

"Night. We should get going."

She wiggled back, pushing my cock deeper inside her. "Then get going, mate. Don't leave me unsatisfied."

Such a tease, and I loved it.

I braced her hips and started moving within her, giving her long, deep strokes that made her gasp out her bliss.

I loved how hot she became for me and how quickly.

And I loved how her clit swelled when I touched it. Which I did. How could I resist fondling that sweet little bud when I knew it drove her crazy?

We moved together slowly. Exquisitely. Coming at the same time and in a flame of bliss so high, it nearly blinded me.

"Mate," I said, tightening my arms around her.

Her fingers traced across my arm. "Mate."

We lay inside the tent as our bodies came down. Eventually, the head of my cock shrunk, and I could slip it from her body.

I wanted to claim her again; be claimed by her. We deserved this and so much more.

Soon, I told myself. Soon we'd be together for always.

We dressed and left the tent, packing it up. After eating, I shouldered the bag while she tucked Rosie inside her shirt, and we continued across the island, aiming for the next section of wasteland, which was shallower than the last. The stepping islands became larger, some taking multiple paces to cross.

By the time we finished the next stretch, we were more than halfway across the wasteland from what I remembered.

With heavy cloud cover, there were no moons to light our way tonight, but we chose not to use our headlamps. By now, the Vessars would be combing the area, seeking, and the lights would draw them to us.

We moved quickly and quietly, helping each other across tough sections.

Then we reached the end of the wetlands. A long desert stretched ahead of us.

"What are the traps in this section? This feels too easy," she whispered when we stopped at the top of a rise. Rosie poked her head out of Charlie's shirt and stared across the broad expanse, remaining quiet, though her little nose twitched.

I stroked her head and she cooed.

Sand stretched ahead of us, coating rolling hills with next to no vegetation.

"We'll have to watch out for holes like the one on the crusty section we first crossed," I said, also worried about how easy this trek had been.

"I assume there are creatures below ground, hoping we'll fall through the surface."

"Unfortunately, yes. I barely avoided being eaten twice while crossing the first time."

Her hand tightened around mine. "Thank you for coming for me. I know I was snarky when you arrived."

"You had a solid reason, and I don't blame you."

"I should've welcomed you with open arms."

My low laugh rang out. "That would've surprised me."

"It's always good to keep you on your toes."

"You make my life better, Charlie. It's brighter and happier."

"Shaede." She leaned against me, and I held her.

Then we stepped out into the desert.

CHAPTER THIRTY-ONE

CHARLIE

We wanted to keep moving in the dark but being unable to see traps would ensure we died quickly. Reluctantly, we turned on our headlamps, though we kept the setting low, generating just enough light to outline a few feet in front of us.

"Look." I pointed to a section of sand subtly swirling to our right, at the base of the hill we were slipping and sliding down. I nudged my chin to another moving piece of ground straight ahead. "Are those the traps you spoke of?"

"Yes." He urged me to the left, where the ground still appeared smooth.

"I assume there's solid ground beneath all the sand."

"Somewhat."

"What does that mean?"

When a section of sand started shifting beneath me, I leaped forward, putting distance between me and it.

A small hole opened. It widened, sucking down sand into a gaping, circular maw full of long, pointy teeth.

I scrambled backward, Shaede beside me. My heart thudded heavily, and my palms flashed with sweat.

I held Rosie against my belly, protecting her, and her soft chitter rang out. She poked her head out the top of my shirt, and her light blue fur stood on end. Her long, slender tail coiled around my wrist, holding tight.

"It's okay, sweetheart," I said. "We'll protect you."

Shaede put his arm around me, lending me assurance, and I was grateful he was here with us. Rosie and I had been a tiny team for a lunar cycle, but it was hard to stand by yourself and face the world with only a pet.

The jaws snapped closed, and the mouth sunk back into the sand, leaving nothing but a smooth area behind.

"What's the best way to get past this section of the wasteland?" I asked.

"Running. If we move fast, the creatures won't have time to spring up to the surface and open their mouths."

"Then we run." I tucked Rosie inside my shirt. "Hang in there, little girl. We're getting out of here."

She chirped and snuggled against my belly.

Shaede took my hand. "Hold tight. Then if something happens . . ."

He meant if a jaw opened and one of us started to slide into the mouth, there was half a chance he could pull me out. He was a lot heavier than me, but I'd find the strength of a superhero if he was the one sliding into the maw.

"It's not going to happen." My voice came out confidently, but I quaked inside. I wasn't afraid of anything except losing him and Rosie. From the time I signed up to work with the interstellar force, I knew my life would often be on the line. We all had to live with it; it came with the job.

But for the first time, I felt I had something—someone—to live for, and I didn't want to lose him.

So I tightened my hand around his and held tight. Nothing and no one was going to tear us apart. I needed to hold fast to that thought, no matter what happened.

We raced across the sand, and it was tough going. Our feet sunk to our ankles, and we were dragged backward with each step up one of the rolling hills. We skidded down the other side, but even then, I felt like we were taking one step back for two steps forward.

I was soon sweaty and breathing hard.

Rosie clung to the inside of my shirt, shivering, as if she knew how dangerous the situation was. She barely moved. I sensed she didn't want to be a distraction.

Sand coiled in circles around us, each opening to gaping jaws eager to gobble us down. The beasts beneath must feel our movement on the surface. It was terrifying. I kept expecting a hole to open exactly where I'd placed my feet.

"You're doing great," Shaede said, and I appreciated his encouragement, as well as his extra boost up each hill. "Keep going. Not long now!"

Sadly, we still had a long stretch ahead, but the forest we aimed for was growing larger.

Maybe we'd make it after all.

No, we *would* make it. I had to trust in that, not let defeat grab hold of me and drag me down.

"You're doing great too," I said. He needed the encouragement as much as I did. He'd been strong throughout this, taking charge right from the start because he believed I needed it.

I was grateful he saw me as an equal now, but that didn't mean he was feeling secure about our situation.

"We'll reach your ship soon, then we're outta here," I said.

He shot me a grin and his steps seemed to lighten. He scooped me into his arms with a laugh and flew up a hill, depositing me at the tip. "Keep up, sweetheart."

My chuckle rang out. "You're the one lagging."

"Lagging, eh? I'll show you lagging."

Excitement poured through me. I couldn't wait to see what he'd do to "show" me. Actually, I knew, and I'd return it to him.

Feeling better about the situation leant me the energy to keep going. I raced past him, giggling; something I hadn't done since I was little.

He caught up, and we raced across the desert, our headlights dancing. We leapt over areas where creatures were rising to the surface, leaving them behind.

Finally, we reached the edge of the sandy area, and the traveling became easier on ground that felt solid. Scruffy grass gave way to scraggly bushes.

We kept going, our steps dragging, but with escape in sight, we both found new energy to keep moving.

"First one to the ship wins," I panted.

"You don't know where the ship is. And even if you did, I'm going to win."

"Cocky."

He snorted. "You're the one who issued the challenge." He pointed. "And the ship is in that direction."

I veered right, aiming for a thick stand of trees. A shadowy shape loomed there, covered with branches. Good job hiding it. If he hadn't pointed it out, I wouldn't have seen it.

I ran harder, adrenaline surging through me now that the end was in sight. I also wanted to beat Shaede because why not?

No matter which of us got there first, we both won.

Shaede's footsteps rang out. He was so close behind me; he could tap my butt with his palm. Show off.

My laughter streamed from me as I raced to the ship. We'd rip off the branches and soar toward the heavens within minues. I couldn't wait to set a course for headquarters. Then we could use the cleansing unit, eat, and climb into bed—bed being the thing I looked forward to the most.

Seeing no hatch on this side, I rounded the tail of the ship and bolted for the middle, neck and neck with Shaede.

I smacked into someone who grabbed me.

Horror dumped through me as I gaped up at Warden Gruxidon.

Clutching my arms, he shook me before tossing me onto the ground. "Yousss made big mistakesss."

When I reached for the knife, he kicked out. It

snapped from my hand, tumbling across the ground, too far out of my reach.

A snarl ripped from the warden's throat, and the Vessar guards clustered behind him laughed. "To prison!" he said. "Now yousss will never escapesss."

CHAPTER THIRTY-TWO

SHAEDE

I pulled the laser pistol, but the warden swept out a claw, knocking it from my hand. Growling, I leaped onto him, determined to take him out of the equation quickly. We'd board the ship and lock him out, and then there would be nothing he could do to keep us from escaping.

He kicked, knocking me to the side, then struck out, raking his claws down my thigh. On his feet, he bellowed and waved for his guards to attack.

There were too many of them. Three or four, I could challenge, but he'd brought at least twenty.

While Charlie cried out in dismay, numerous guards piled on top of me, quickly pinning me to the ground. I got in a few blows, but in no time, my hands were bound behind me, and my ankles were weighed down with manacles.

They loaded us into different skimmers and flew us back toward the prison.

I hated seeing the hard-earned progress we'd made negated. We'd put a lot of work into crossing each section of the wasteland.

This felt like defeat, but I wouldn't give up so easily. Yes, they'd bound us. But we'd find a way to get free again, and the next time, we'd escape the planet.

Assuming my ship remained where it was. Would they send equipment to bring it to the prison? If so, that might make things easier. We could fly away from the prison yard itself.

As the skimmer coasted up over the gate and landed in the open area of the compound, I spied something odd in front of the partly destroyed prison.

They'd erected posts, and Pralk hung from chains secured to the top.

Damn, they'd caught him.

"Prison sssecure," the warden said. He kicked out, hitting my thigh with the tip of his boot, making the wounds he'd left with his claws start seeping blood again. Pain swept through me, threatening to drown me, but I bit it back, shoving it to the farthest reaches of my mind. I couldn't give in. I had to stay alert so that when our chance came, we could take it. "No escapesss. Ever." His slick grin rose. "As for femalesss . . ."

"Leave her alone," I growled.

He studied my face. "Who are yousss?"

"Someone who stumbled into the prison by mistake."

"You came heresss," he snarled, sitting bolt upright. "You came for hersss."

I wasn't saying a damn thing about Charlie. "Don't know her."

"Yet, yousss with her." His gaze shot to the skimmer landing beside ours. "I ask hersss."

"I told you to leave her alone."

He cackled, the sound of his laughter clawing down my spine. "I do what I wishesss. I rule heresss." He studied my face. "What willsss you do to protect hersss?"

Anything, but I wouldn't name it. He must know we were at least friends. That was clear by us escaping together. He'd caught us again together at the mine and bound us for supposed punishment.

"If you hurt her, she won't mine for you," I said.

"Hasss enough brugeer," he said with scorn. "Need no moresss."

"Gems."

"Do not need gemsss."

I wouldn't name the stripeene. He'd guessed so much; it would be foolish to let him know what we'd discovered.

He rose to his feet. "Comesss." Tipping his head back, he laughed again. "No choice, rightsss?"

The hatch opened, and he descended, flicking a claw back to where I lay bound on the floor. "Takesss him to cell."

Guards scrambled up the ramp and hefted me off the floor of the skimmer, half-dragging me outside. I looked around but didn't see Charlie. What had they done with her?

The warden stomped toward the partly destroyed

prison building, only stopping to gloat at Pralk. "Diesss soon. All diesss!"

Not if I had anything to say about it.

Guards hauled Charlie from another skimmer, and she looked my way with quiet desperation.

I swore she mouthed something to me, but I couldn't be sure.

Watch for it?

She couldn't have anything else planned. We'd used up her supplies and made it across the wasteland. Anything else she might've arranged for had happened already.

They hauled her into the prison building, and she walked with them, not fighting. The slight bulge in her shirt told me Rosie had made it through all right. Would the tiny creature run once they were securely inside?

Guards carried me toward the open doorway.

As I passed Pralk, our gazes met. I found strength in his eyes, telling me he still had plenty of fight left in him.

I gave him a sharp nod, and he responded with a slick grin.

"Watch and wait, my friend," I whispered with determination blasting through my core. "We're going to end this."

CHAPTER THIRTY-THREE

CHARLIE

Pralk's bomb hadn't destroyed enough of the prison. A few of the cells had collapsed, but there were plenty of others left to house everyone, though some inmates would probably have to bunk with others.

They dumped me in the same cell I'd been in originally and slammed the door shut. I'd yet to see the warden, but I was sure he'd be by soon to sneer.

Fear kept trying to overwhelm me. They knew I was female, and women never fared well in a prison.

They left me bound at my wrists and ankles. Squirming, I was able to sit up on my bunk, my back to the wall and my knees drawn to my chest. I kept shivering from reaction. And tears stung in the back of my eyes. We'd been so close to escaping. So near to ending this for good.

Rosie poked her head out of my shirt and looked up at me, her whiskered nose wiggling.

"How are we going to get out of here, sweetie?" I

whispered. "Pralk's plan to take over the prison failed. Shaede and I were caught. They know I'm not a boy. The pin I used to open my cell is on the other side of the wasteland." Everything felt insurmountable. "I have no way of escaping this cell. It feels so hopeless." I knew my dejection partly came from being worn out, but my heart ached. "I love Shaede so much, and I can't help him. I can't even help myself."

My eyes stung again, but I held back my tears. They'd do nothing for me, and while it might be silly, I didn't want to lose that tiny bit of water. Who knew when they'd give me something to drink?

Rosie wiggled close to my neck and nuzzled it, offering comfort I needed so much. If only I could hug her and give her pats. She'd been an amazing friend when I needed one most.

After looking up at me again for a long minue, she released a low chitter, and I swore she nodded.

She scooted out of my shirt and leapt onto the floor. Like other times, she slid between the bars and scurried down the hall, probably looking for her next meal.

My rumbling belly told me it would like some food, too, but I doubted any would be forthcoming.

I'd been cocky when I told Shaede to watch for it, because I had no other plans.

How was I going to get us out of this trap? They'd tied Pralk out front, displaying him for all to see. A warning not to try to escape. The other prisoners would take heed.

Not me and not Shaede. We had to get out of here, but how?

They placed Shaede in a cell a few down from mine. I scrambled to my feet and hobbled to the bars between us, watching as they dropped him onto his bunk, bound at his ankles and wrists like me. Blood coated his right thigh where the warden had clawed him.

"He needs his wound tended," I cried, but the guards ignored me, locking Shaede's cell and stomping down the hall to the partly crumbled staircase. Only that end of the building had sustained damage and not enough to make a difference. I wasn't sure what went wrong, but it hardly mattered now.

The plan had fallen apart. Pralk and his friends were supposed to use the distraction of the bomb to take down the guards, then gain control of the prison.

I needed to figure out something I could do other than sit on my bunk and mourn. When life threw you rotten tomatoes, you had a few choices. You could stomp on them, eat them, ignore them, or . . .

I was sure something good was supposed to end the saying, but I couldn't figure it out.

Sighing, I hobbled back and forth in the small cell, my footsteps a low shuffle.

A tiny sound in the hall sent me to the front bars, and I spied Rosie scurrying my way. Something made a tap-tap-tap sound, but I couldn't place it.

She stopped outside my cell and dropped whatever she carried, looking up at me. Her cheerful chitter echoed in the hall as she nudged it forward.

A master key to the cells and manacles. The last time I saw it, it was hanging on a chain from the warden's belt.

I stretched my arm between the bars and grabbed the key.

"Baby cakes, you are amazing," I whispered.

She tipped her little pointy nose in the air and wiggled with joy, preening.

In no time, I'd unlocked my bindings and the door to my cell. I tiptoed down the hall, making almost no sound, and unlocked Shaede's cell too.

He rolled over as I approached him, his eyes widening with shock.

I held up the key. "Would you like to be handcuffed together again, or shall we do this without being bound?"

He grinned. "I did enjoy being cuffed to you, sweetheart." When he held out his hands, I unlocked his manacles, then the ones securing his ankles. He leaped from the bunk and lifted me off my feet, whirling me around before giving me a long, hot kiss that didn't last anywhere near enough.

"You're wonderful," he said, holding me as I slid down his body until my feet touched the ground.

"Thank Rosie. She's clever. We should recommend her services to the head of the agency."

"Or at least make sure she has an honorary role."

I scooped her up and gave her a quick hug.

"Let me look at your leg," I said, frowning at the gashes peeking through the torn material of his pants.

"I'm fine."

"You were bleeding." I dropped down and moved the material until I could examine each slice. "Not bleeding now." The skin around the wounds was puffy and a little red. Same with the bite mark from the creature in the small cave below the wasteland. With a good cleaning and antibiotics, he'd heal up nicely. All the more reason to get out of here. "I can wrap it."

He tugged me up. "Leave it. We can take care of it later. I'll be all right until then."

I worried my lower lip with my teeth and finally sighed. "Okay. But if it starts hurting, tell me and we'll find a way to make it feel better."

He nodded and took my hand, tugging me to the door of his cell.

We jogged down the hall and took the rickety stairs that held our weight. At the ground level, we peered through a crack in the door, finding no one on the other side. The other inmates must still be mining.

Voices echoed, moving away from us.

I darted into the hall and slunk close to a window looking out at the center of the prison.

Shaede joined me. "They're moving more stripeene."

Vehicles rumbled across the compound and out the gate.

"They're no longer making an effort to hide what they're doing."

"Maybe the warden knows he won't get away with it for long, so he's making sure he maximizes his profits."

"Pralk's watching too."

"They won't let him tell anyone."

My heart froze. Pralk had been a friend when I needed one most. "We can't let them kill him."

"Don't plan to."

I turned toward him. "What can we do? We can't sneak out there when they're coming and going."

He frowned and tapped his chin. "We'll need to provide a distraction."

"What do you have in mind?" I asked.

"Explosives will only take you so far." His eyes sparkled with unexpected humor. "I'm not sure you'll be willing to go along with it."

"Spill it, *boss*."

His chuckle rang out. "What do you think about providing a little entertainment instead?"

"My voice is horrible," I said, unsure about this plan Shaede had cooked up.

"As hot as you look right now, sweetheart, it won't matter how good your voice is."

I pursed my lips at him and picked at the sheer drapery I'd coiled around my naked body. "I'm not sure about this."

His mood sobered. We'd raided one of the little used offices—as evidenced by the dust—and took down the curtains. I'd stripped and wrapped one around myself, leaving most of my skin exposed.

"We can do something else, then," he said.

"Like what?" I propped a hand on my hip. "Maybe they're not interested in humans. They could be turned on only by Vessar lizard ladies. I don't have a single scale or claw. But it's the only plan we can come up with."

"You're gorgeous." He tugged me into his arms. "They'd be blind not to notice."

"I guess this could work." Truly, we didn't have much to go with. We needed to free Pralk before they killed him, and Shaede wanted to get into the building where they were combining the stripeene with tetradivon. He had a plan that he hadn't shared. I had a feeling that things were about to get loud within the compound. "I'll do it."

Stepping back, he took my hands, squeezing them. "Just draw their attention, then disappear. Hide in the basement with the pool. I'll come for you once this is over."

I sucked in a breath and released it. Once I stepped outside, my clothing would be left behind. If I ran back here, they'd catch me, and I didn't want to think about what they might do if they did enjoy a human female's body as much as a lizard's.

"You're right," I said. "I need to hide."

"We can do this." He pressed a fist against his chest where his hearts beat for me. "I won't let them hurt you. I promise."

I gave him a nod and curled my finger toward him until he bent close enough for a lingering kiss. "We need alone time. Soon."

"I promise you'll get that as well, mate." He flashed

me a grin that faded too fast before tapping my ass with his big palm. "Go. I won't be far behind."

CHAPTER THIRTY-FOUR
SHAEDE

I walked with her to the front door, grateful they'd taken all the guards to help with the stripeene operation.

After another kiss, I stroked her face. "Be safe and run fast, mate."

"I won't let them catch me."

So brave. Fear lingered in her eyes, but she didn't voice it. She knew I'd do anything to protect her, but in this, I had to thrust her into danger.

"See you soon," she said with a forced smile. Lifting Rosie from where she sat by Charlie's feet, she nuzzled her face against the creature. "Stay here, little one. I'll come back for you, but I want you safe."

I wasn't sure the little beastie could understand, but Charlie explained how the rodent went off alone and located the master key, and brought it to her so what did I know? This creature could be more intelligent than all of us combined.

After lowering Rosie to the floor, Charlie gave me one last look full of love. Then she opened the door and slipped outside.

Rosie looked up at me and chittered before scooting toward the opening, following Charlie. I tried to grab her, though I had no idea where I could put her to keep her safe. The rodent sensed my intentions and ran faster, scrambling through the door.

Grumbling, I peered through a crack in the opening, watching as Charlie tiptoed to the right and around a building. Rosie followed, though some distance behind.

Charlie would come at the Vessars from the far right, drawing their attention in that direction.

"They call me the queen of the ball," she sang out in a loud voice.

A few Vessars barked, and one of the trucks leaving the stripeene processing building came to a quick halt. Vessars poured from the cab, their wide eyes focused on the direction where Charlie kept singing about dancing at the ball with a handsome prince. I hoped we'd have a chance to dance together after we escaped this planet. We'd brief the agency, then our time would belong to us.

I wouldn't waste the opportunity she was giving me. With the master key in hand, I slunk out the door and to the left, aiming for the open area where they'd strung up Pralk.

He dangled, his body limp, and I wondered if it was already too late. He wasn't a vital part of our plan, but we couldn't leave him here to be killed.

Peering past the building, I watched the Vessars flowing en masse toward Charlie. Our plan was working too well.

As much as I wanted to race in her direction and shield her with my own body, I had to continue with the task I'd taken on. I left the shadows of the building and ran toward Pralk.

His head lifted as I approached, and he hissed with joy.

I unfastened his manacles, and he drooped in my arms. But he quickly straightened.

"Hasss water?" he asked in a scratchy voice.

I handed him the flask we'd found in a small galley partway down the hall, plus a bit of wrapped food. "We can't stay here long."

"Then we run." After gulping down some water and refastening the flask, he peered around me, his body stiffening. "Where isss Charlie?" His face froze. "No. She singsss?"

Her voice lilted toward us, though it sounded far away and jolts rang through it. Good, she was running. With luck, she'd soon be hidden where they wouldn't find her.

When Pralk started in that direction, I grabbed his arm.

"How would you like to help me end this once and for all?" I asked.

Pralk growled, his eyes gleaming with excitement. "What we dosss?"

"Follow me." With him on my heels, I ran toward the back of the building where they mixed stripeene and tetradivon.

CHAPTER THIRTY-FIVE

CHARLIE

I *really* couldn't sing, but the Vessars didn't seem upset about my voice. Their gazes remained locked on my body as they sauntered toward me, their pencil-thin tongues flicking out and their tails swishing lazily behind them. They thought I was theirs for the taking, and they were eager to get started.

My only concern—well, one of my concerns—was that I didn't see the warden. Where was he?

When the rest of the Vessars were fifteen feet or so away, I turned and wiggled my ass. Their hissing grew louder. Cringing, I bolted toward the door to the equipment building. I ran fast and was grateful I somehow remained ahead of the guards. They yipped and snarled behind me, shouting out what they planned to do with me once they caught me.

I hit the equipment storage building and wrenched open the door, startling a Vessar standing just inside. A shove, and he toppled backward, landing hard on the floor. I raced past him, streaking through the big room, weaving around tractors and broken equipment. The door banged open behind me, and the Vessars poured inside, shouting, some galloping on four legs.

I flung myself through the far door, not pausing to see if anyone lurked outside. It didn't matter who caught me, the Vessars inside or potential guards out here.

My heart thundering, I flew across the open area and flung open the door to the building housing the hidden pool.

Inside, I rushed to the closet and ducked down through the hatch in the floor.

I stood in the dark below, struggling to contain my panting, listening.

Yells rang out, but I couldn't tell if they came from above or from the yard.

When stomps echoed overhead, I cringed against the wall. A sharp look around showed there was no place to hide and no exit other than back out the way I'd arrived.

My skin crawled when the footsteps grew closer. They couldn't know about my hiding spot. Please.

The hatch above was wrenched open, and a Vessar stuffed his head into the gap.

"Theresss isss," he said with a slick grin.

He hopped down through the hole and while others did the same, the first rushed toward me.

I kicked out, hitting him hard in the guts, and he stumbled backward. While he righted himself, I raced across the room.

Someone grabbed me from behind, hauling me

against his scaled body. His hands clamped down hard on me, his claws digging into my throat.

"Holdsss still," he hissed by my ear.

I stomped down on the top of his foot, but he only grunted and didn't release me.

I shrieked, flailing, but I couldn't get free.

He lifted me and tossed me to one of his friends who immediately did the same. They passed me across the room while I shrieked and struck out with my fists.

I was handed up to Vessars waiting at the top. They quickly pinned my hands behind my back and secured my ankles, giving me only about a foot of leash to walk with.

One of the guards hefted me over his shoulder and stomped toward the exit, the rest streaming behind us, catcalling.

Outside, the guard continued to where they'd pinned Pralk, and while I was glad to see he no longer hung from the posts, I couldn't tell if they'd removed him because he'd died or if Shaede had been able to complete that part of our plan.

The warden wasn't in sight, but that didn't mean he wasn't somewhere nearby.

With a grunt, the guard tossed me onto the ground. The wind was knocked from my lungs, but I scrambled to rise. Before I could leap to my feet, a guard grabbed my wrists from behind and pinned me to the ground.

Others crowded around, their tongues flicking, their eyes full of eagerness. Shit, shit, shit.

"Holdsss her," the one who appeared to be in charge said.

He stepped forward while others grappled for my ankles.

Rosie leaped from behind me, landing on his face. Her tiny claws dug in, and he shrieked, spinning. Reaching up, he wrenched her off and tossed her aside.

I kicked, screaming her name, trying to break free, but the guard holding me only tightened his grip.

"Rosie," I cried. "Rosie!"

The head guard rushed toward me . . .

And the world exploded around us.

CHAPTER THIRTY-SIX

SHAEDE

Pralk and I set things up and hauled ass out of the building housing the altered stripeene. They'd moved most of it, but there was enough left behind.

A commotion in the middle of the compound drew my attention. At least fifteen guards crowded around something lying on the ground. I didn't need to look to know what they were salivating over.

With a nod to Pralk, I pulled the laser pistols I'd located inside the stripeene building and raced toward Charlie. Pralk followed, growling, though he veered toward the prison when I waved him off.

When it came to protecting my mate, I could handle a few guards.

The building behind us exploded, tossing me forward.

I rolled along the ground and came up fast, still running toward my mate. A feral rage burned inside me.

I'd protect her. Die for her. Rip apart anyone who caused her harm.

The guards crowding around her scattered, though I doubted it was because they were worried about me. They gaped at the building that was quickly being consumed by flames.

Another explosion blasted past us, this one taking down the entire front section of the wall. The rest of the enclosure rippled and started crumbling.

While the rest of the front wall toppled, the guards bolted for the main prison building, leaving Charlie lying on the ground. They'd soon be surprised by Pralk and the non-mining inmates he'd gone ahead to free. I anticipated Pralk's original plan to take over the prison would succeed this time.

Charlie jumped to her feet and looked ready to run until she saw me rushing toward her. With a happy cry, she hobbled my way.

I caught her and lifted her, spinning her around before backing toward the equipment building I'd left untouched. Removing my shirt, I helped her put it on, so she was covered to her mid-thighs.

"Rosie," she cried, scrambling until I put her down. "Rosie!"

Charlie's little rodent friend cheeped from across the compound and raced toward her, jumping into her arms. I held them both as the buildings burned.

Pralk and the inmates streamed from the prison, and they quickly subdued the stunned guards who'd survived the wall's collapse.

Skimmers arrived from the mines and the prisoners walked around the destroyed gate, gaping in wonder, while Pralk and a few of his friends approached me and Charlie.

"It'sss over," Pralk said with a grin. "I am in charge."

"What do you plan to do now?" I asked. I trusted him because Charlie did, but if he was going to take over the stripeene operation, I couldn't allow that.

"Gemsss. Brugeer," he said. His hand swept out to encompass the others. "We make moneysss. Sendsss to familiesss."

"They plan to run a regular business," Charlie said. She handed Rosie to me, then hobbled forward and hugged Pralk, whose eyes widened. He awkwardly patted her back before releasing her bindings. She stepped away from him and back into my arms.

Rosie seemed content with me, which made me grin. She was a friend to us both now.

"How will you keep the Vessars from sending enforcements to take back the prison?" I asked, patting Rosie's little head.

"Let themsss try," Pralk said with grim satisfaction. He hefted his fist and the rest of the inmates cheered. "I contact family inside, and family sendsss help. I now rulesss this planet."

Ruled?

No matter. I'd make sure the agency sent some help. We needed allies among the Vessars, so why not start with Pralk and his friends?

Pralk's head cocked, and he frowned as if he was just

now noticing how Charlie was dressed, plus her long hair hanging down her back. "How I think yousss littlesss brother?"

"I'm sorry I didn't tell you who I am," she said, wincing.

Pralk nodded. "Is fine. Safersss." His gaze took us both in. "What doesss now?"

"If you don't mind," I said. "We'll take a skimmer to my ship. You can pick the skimmer up there or leave it."

"Very wellsss," Pralk said. His gaze fell on Charlie again. "Will miss you, friend."

She hugged him again. "Keep in touch?"

"Yes, broth— err, sssister."

CHAPTER THIRTY-SEVEN

CHARLIE

I dressed in my own clothing quickly while Shaede commandeered a skimmer.

"I still can't believe it's over," I said as I took the driver's seat, handing him back his shirt. Interestingly enough, Shaede offered to sit in the other seat and hold Rosie, who we were taking with us.

I loved seeing her gazing up at him with adoration while he patted her soft fur.

"Ready?" I asked as the hatch closed and I powered up the skimmer.

Shaede held out his hand. When our palms connected, he lifted my hand and kissed it, giving me a quick nod. "Get us out of here, mate. It's over."

We'd notify Interstellar Interpol, and they'd come in to clean up whatever might be left from the stripeene operation. They'd also send spies into the other prisons to see if they were up to the same business as the warden.

Later, we'd send Pralk assistance, though I was confident my friend would be able to rebuild the prison into something better all on his own. They were already talking about residences and sending word to their home planet for their mates and families to come join them. In no time, the prison would be transformed into a community.

I was going to miss my friend, but I would visit.

Compressing the shift, I guided the skimmer up and over the crumbling ruins of the gate. We soon soared across the wasteland, and I marveled at how little time it took to reach the other side.

I landed the skimmer near Shaede's ship, and we exited the vehicle.

Rosie leapt from Shaede's arms into mine and nuzzled my neck.

"Are you ready to leave this planet, little one?" I asked.

She chittered, and Shaede and I shared a grin.

"I can't believe it's finally over," I said as we walked toward the ship's hatch. "We destroyed the Vessar mafia explosive operation and took down their prison. It's going to be hard to top something like that."

"You will notsss," someone hissed behind us.

We spun around to find Warden Gruxidon stomping toward us from the nearby tree line. He crossed the open area with a laser pistol pointed at my head.

Shaede grabbed my arm and tucked me behind him. We started backing toward the ship, but with the hatch closed, I doubted we could get inside before the warden shot us.

"It's over, Warden," I said. "The prison is destroyed and Pralk is in charge. Give up, and we'll see you safely from the planet." Not in Shaede's ship, but there was no reason to tell him that.

"No safe passagesss," he said with a scowl. "You diesss." He tightened his grip on the gun.

A shadow passed overhead and hovered over the warden, followed by a transport beam stabbing down to the ground.

My brother, Matis, appeared beneath the ship in the beam, right behind the warden. He stepped forward and pressed the barrel of a laser gun against the warden's head.

Growing up, I'd envied my brother's burnished bronze skin, his dark hair shot through with silver, and his big, muscular form. He was strong and ruthless, and I was never happier to see him than now.

"Drop the weapon," he growled.

No one ignored that deep, assertive voice. Not if they valued their life.

The warden's hand shook, but he kept his weapon pointed at my head. "No."

My brother shot, hitting the warden from behind, and the Vessar stumbled forward, collapsing on the ground. Matis kicked the weapon from the warden's hand, and I snatched it up and tucked it into the back of my pants, juggling Rosie in my other hand.

I handed her to Shaede and raced around the warden's body, jumping into my big brother's arms.

He held me, grinning. "Well, little sis. Nice to see you too." He snarled at the warden's body. "Looks like I got here just in time."

"We were handling the situation," I said, my lips twisting. I leaned against his chest. "No need to rub it in."

He put me down and walked over to slap Shaede's arm. "Well done, friend. Well done."

"Hey," I said. "I was part of this operation too."

My brother turned and grimaced. "You were kidnapped. I couldn't come to you, and I didn't know if you were dead or alive."

"I was working my way through it."

"She was," Shaede said. "She would've escaped even if I hadn't rescued her."

"We rescued each other," I pointed out.

Matis looked back and forth between us, his brow furrowing.

"Do you want a ride anywhere?" he asked, his glance taking in the small ship.

"That's mine," Shaede said with pride. "We'll leave the planet with it."

"Then I'll return to what I was already doing," Matis said. Spy work, then.

"How did you know we needed you at this minue?" I asked, curious.

His gaze flicked away from mine. "That's classified."

"Ah. I see." I took in the dinged-up ship he'd arrived

in that reminded me of vehicles I'd seen parked on rickety platforms during some of my shadier assignments. My brother had been working undercover as a space pirate and was clearly still on assignment. If anything, Matis enjoyed nice things. He'd only fly in a trap like this if he had to.

"If you don't need a ride, then, I'll get going," he said. "Will I see you at the orphanage for the holidays?"

"We wouldn't miss it."

"We . . ." Something shifted out from behind his neck. Had it been clinging to his back?

I frowned at the blue and white fluffy creature about the length of my forearm. "What's that?"

"*That* is my friend," Matis said, stroking the little beasty that vaguely resembled the cats I remembered from Earth. Its long claws and the sharp point on its tail suggested it might be an interstellar hybrid. "And his name is Snuggles. He was injured. Crying. I couldn't leave him."

That was Matis, always adopting strays, including me.

"Snuggles?" I snickered.

"It's a long story." He scowled. "Besides, it fits."

"If you say so."

The space kitty rubbed its face against Matis, and he scooped it up, flipped it over, and held it like a baby in his arms while rubbing its belly.

"You two don't get along very well, do you?" I said, grinning so wide my face ached.

Matis's scowl deepened as he scratched Snuggles

under the chin. The creature's eyes slid shut, and his rough purr echoed around us. "What do you mean?"

"Nothing." I snickered. "Nothing."

I grinned up at Shaede, and he put his arm around me, tugging me against his side. I sighed and leaned into his embrace.

"So, you two finally straightened things out?" Matis asked with a low laugh, his gaze sliding from Shaede to me. He flipped Snuggles back up onto his shoulder, and the little beastie sat, watching us with big, unearthly blue eyes, twitching its whiskers.

"Finally?" I asked, leaning against my mate.

Matis shrugged. "I always knew you two should be together. I couldn't figure out why you didn't see it yaros ago."

"*I* did," I said, poking my mate's side. "It just took Shaede a bit longer to come to the same conclusion."

Shaede put Rosie on his shoulder, and she struck a pose similar to Snuggles's, watching the other creature with curiosity in her eyes.

Shaede's arm tightened around me, and he leaned over to kiss my forehead. "I did take too long, mate. You're right, as always. But one thing is clear. You're mine, and there's no escaping me now."

"As long as you know you're mine too," I said. "All mine. Don't ever forget it."

He lifted me off my feet, and his lips hovered over mine. "Trust me. I never will, mate."

And then he kissed me.

CHAPTER THIRTY-EIGHT

EPILOGUE: CHARLIE

I waved as my brother's ship took off.

"What are we going to do about the warden's body?" I asked.

"I'll send word to Pralk. He can take care of it."

Or not. Why would he bother? It felt odd just leaving the body here, though I imagine the warden would've done the same with me and Shaede.

"Are you ready to leave now, mate?" Shaede asked. He pressed a few buttons on the side of the ship, and the hatch opened.

"More than ready. You said something about a cleansing unit on your ship?" I couldn't wait to feel clean again and dress in something I hadn't worn for dias, even if it wasn't my size.

"It's a big cleansing unit," he said, his arm around me as we strolled up the ramp and inside the small ship. "I'm sure there's room for two."

The hatch shut, and I put Rosie on her feet. Her

whiskers twitched, and with a chirp, she raced down the hall toward the bridge. If I knew my little friend, she'd make herself at home in no time.

"Show me to the cleanser," I said with a sly smile. "I'm feeling rather dirty."

He bent forward and nuzzled my neck. "Maybe I like you dirty."

We helped each other out of our clothing, kissing as we did it and leaving a trail of shirts and pants in the hall.

Inside the small bathing chamber, I turned on the cleanser and stepped inside. He was right, there was enough room for two.

Grinning, I coiled my finger his way, watching as he sauntered in my direction. "I might get clean, but for you, love, I'm more than happy to get dirty."

I hope you enjoyed Charlie & Shaede's
story! I've always wanted to write a prison
planet romance, and now I have!

Would you like to visit with Charlie
& Shaede one more time?
Sign up for my newsletter &
receive a bonus scene.
Shaede and Charlie have a surprise . . .

Next up is Matis & Tatum's story,
When Tatum sneaks on board a pirate
spaceship and accidentally stabs the captain,
he makes her work as his cabin boy.
Good thing he doesn't realize she's female...
Pick up your copy of Pirating the Alien now!
I've included the first chapter here . . .

ABOUT THE AUTHOR

Ava Ross is a two-time *USA Today* Bestselling author who has written numerous titles, all of them featuring sweet and steamy romance. She fell for men with unusual features when she first watched Star Wars, where alien creatures have gone mainstream. She lives in New England with her husband (who is sadly not an alien, though he is still cute in his own way), her kids, and a few assorted pets.

SERIES BY AVA

Mail-Order Brides of Crakair

Brides of Driegon

Fated Mates of the Ferlaern Warriors

Fated Mates of the Xilan Warriors

Holiday with a Cu'zod Warrior

Galaxy Games

Alien Warrior Abandoned/
Shattered Galaxies

Beastly Alien Boss

Bride of the Fae

A Sci-Fi Holiday Tail

Monsterville, USA
(Includes Monster Between the Sheets &
Sweet Monster Treats)

Monster on Board
(co-written with Alana Khan)

You can find my books on Amazon.

PIRATING THE ALIEN

I'm falling for my space pirate boss, but rogue aliens are after him—and now me.

It was a simple job. Sneak aboard a pirate spaceship and steal a precious artifact from the brooding, too-hot captain, Matis. Before I know it, I'll be on my way back to Earth with enough credits to cure my mom's sickness.

Is it my fault I accidentally stab him? Instead of making me walk the interstellar plank, he makes me serve as his cabin boy. Good thing he doesn't realize I'm not a boy.

His snarly outside hides a squishy center, but someone's out to kill him, and who needs to get tangled up in that? Then we're trapped on a rogue space station with alien pirates trying to kill us.

He discovers my secret.

He says we'll escape—and then he's claiming me as his fated mate.

Pirating the Alien is Book 7 of the Beastly Alien Boss Series. Each book is standalone and only loosely connected. They can be read in any order. Expect strong women and heroes who are battle-ready, who talk dirty, and who will do everything to be with their fated mates.

Get your copy NOW!

CHAPTER 1
TATUM

When you wake each morning to your mom hacking her lungs out, and the doctors tell you her terminal genetic malformation can be easily cured with a sizeable amount of credits, you'll lie, steal, and maybe even kill to get that cure.

My regular job paid me a decent wage, but it would never be enough for a bill like that. Mom had been sick a very long time. I couldn't stand by and watch her die, not when I could do something about it.

I went to the Interstellar Employment Agency to find a better-paying job, and they gave me three offers. I wasn't interested in being a nanny to two hellion alien younglings, and the thought of massaging the legs of a hundred-legged Vellicore twice a day didn't hold much appeal. But the mystery of the third job intrigued me. That and the huge salary I'd be paid for a short period of time.

Leaving Mom with all the credits I had and enough

medicine for almost a full lunar cycle, I promised to return to her as soon as I could. I was transported to the Plushier Space Station, where I was directed by my wrist com to a secluded location to meet up with my new boss.

The Ergeepelon alien wasn't one for chatting. He laid it out the second I introduced myself.

"You need sneak onto spaceship," he said in choppy universal language. Shifting his six limbs, he kept his face in shadows. His segmented exoskeleton scraped and ground against his other body parts, and the taint of rotting flesh drifted off his shell, hitting my sinuses like I'd stuffed garbage up there.

"That's it? Sneak on board a spaceship?" I panted through my mouth, but I could almost *taste* him. "How am I supposed to do that?"

"We send you in supply capsule. Bots on Skaros Space Station pull you in. When hatch open, you climb out. Seek this ship." He tapped my wrist com—the one they'd sent when I was hired—with a spiked claw, and a name appeared.

"Snuggles?" I asked in amazement. "Who in the galaxy names a starship something like that?"

"Captain."

I shrugged; it hardly mattered what the ship was called.

"Recommend not let them see you," the Ergeepelon lisped, tilting his long, triangular head, watching me with his three black eyes. "They pirates. Slit throat."

I'd take a pass on that.

"Isn't Skaros a floating pile of space junk?" I wasn't

sure about this assignment. There was something he wasn't telling me. "Last I heard, they were having gravity and oxygen problems."

A growl ripped through his segmented body. "They fix all problems." He poked my chest with both of his front limbs, the spikes causing pain even if they didn't break the skin. I'd irritated him. The thought of angering him made my heart seize. "Once on board, find safe in main stateroom, steal artifact."

"What kind of artifact?"

My new com flashed the image of a stone statue about the height and width of my forearm depicting an alien lady in a long flowing gown, her pleading gaze pointed toward the heavens. "Why is this so valuable to you?"

"No question. Want credits? Do job."

The job didn't sound too challenging, and I did need the credits. "Once I have the statue in my position, how will I get it to you?"

"Tap com. We extract."

Sounded easy enough. "Last I heard, Skaros was completely lawless." I was no pirate. My self-defense skills were limited. Okay, non-existent. "What's keeping someone from killing me before I reach the spaceship?"

"Be very careful."

That was a given.

Mom's gasping cough echoed in my mind, shoving aside my urge to tell this alien no. There was more to this mission than he was sharing.

Before I could question him further, he spun and

scurried down the hall, disappearing into the flickering blackness.

To reach the Skaros Space Station, I opted to ride in stasis rather than subject myself to the tubes necessary to manage excretion while lying awake in a capsule for even such a short time.

Thankfully, new tech meant it only took two days to travel half a light year, which was confusing if you dwelled on it too long, so I didn't.

I woke to a black tube surrounding my pod. A grinding, churning sound told me I was being pulled onto Skaros. Good. Things were going just as expected. It shouldn't take long to board the ship, steal the artifact, and activate my com. I'd be on my way back to Earth by the end of the day with enough money to cure Mom.

The capsule came to a jarring halt, and lights bloomed around me. Bangs rang out when the station's outer hatch doors slammed shut. Mechanical arms opened the top of my pod, and I bailed over the side.

A quick check showed the knife I'd strapped to my waist was still with me. It wasn't much, but I was no crack shot with a laser pistol. I might live in a city where laser shootouts were a regular occurrence, but I once read knives and fists were the easiest weapons in a pinch.

Since I wasn't much of a fighter, I usually turned and bolted.

I wasn't stupid. Skaros was a pirate port floating in space. Anything could happen to a slip of an Earthling woman like me—hence me dressing like a boy and strapping on a blade. With shorn hair, bound breasts, and loose, nondescript clothing, I'd pass casual scrutiny and have a way to defend myself if I slipped up and was discovered.

With my heart thumping heavily, I zipped around droids dismantling the capsule. Each part would find a new home, including me on Snuggles. I still couldn't believe a pirate named their spaceship something like that.

In no time, I was weaving through the main section of the space station. Sweaty aliens crowded around me, their skin, scales, and fur overheating from the solar rays shooting through the clear top of the structure. Three suns shone down on the port, and the management had taken advantage of them to generate passive heat. Panels on the outer walls gathered rays to generate power.

I could only identify a quarter of the species around me. Everyone wore weapons and a flinty challenge filled their eyes. Most clutched bags holding their worldly possessions, snarling at anyone who came near enough to try to steal.

In the city where I grew up, a pickpocket caught in action might be fined. Here, they'd lose their hand or head, the alien doling out the punishment without bothering to call the authorities—assuming there were any on board. It was easier to deal with it themselves.

"Snuggles," I whispered into my com. "Where is Snuggles docked?" My com should be able to tap into Skaros's mainframe computer and locate the ship.

Bingo. Directions flashed on the screen along with a convenient map with a blinking dot indicating the spaceship.

I scooted around those selling wares and a few tussles with fur and bits of claws flying, leaping over the carcass of a downed alien at least twice. Drugged or dead, I couldn't determine, and I wasn't about to tap on shoulders to find out.

My com notified me Snuggles was getting ready to depart the port.

Bolting toward where it was docked, adrenaline gave me wings. I flew past aliens trying to grab my attention and scurried away from those who slashed out when I inadvertently knocked them into storefronts.

A minue later, I skidded into the hangar and ducked behind a pile of storage containers, watching as a droid crew finished loading the ship. Lo and behold—Snuggles was written in swirly script on the side of the ship.

How was I going to get on board? Back on the Plushier Space Station, this job sounded relatively easy. Now, I wasn't sure. But I couldn't back out now. There'd be no return ticket until I had the statue in hand.

I watched the droids zipping up and down the ramp loaded with boxes. Eventually, the piles of supplies waiting nearby had been brought on board. I'd yet to see any people working on the ship. Had I lucked out with a ship run solely by machines? Most droids were programmed to complete tasks. They'd ignore anything and anyone else as long as they didn't interfere with the mission. I could stroll on board among them without a care.

When the station droids finished, they filed out of the loading dock.

I took a chance, dashing across the open area between the shipping containers and the ship, and raced up the ramp. At the top, I peered around and, seeing no one, I spied a door marked Janitor's Closet halfway down the hall on my left.

Time to hide until the ship left port. I'd wait until night, creep out and find the main stateroom, steal the artifact, and activate my com. Easy.

The door whisked open at my touch, and I tumbled inside, tangling among various cleaning tools and products and nearly smacking my head on the inner wall.

After clearing a small place on the floor with the side of my foot, I dropped down, scrunched my legs up to my chest, and wrapped my arms around them. I waited for the ship to leave Skaros. Until I could determine if anyone live worked on board, it paid to be cautious. No need to rush to the stateroom and get caught.

It wasn't long before the low rumble of destar generators told me the ship was unhooking from the dock. A floaty feeling made my belly surge up into my throat, but I shoved it back down with a swallow.

A weightless feeling told me the ship drifted away

from Skaros. This was followed by the engines engaging. The room vibrated subtly, making the cleaning tools rattle, reminding me I rode in a pirate ship, not a smooth charter spacecraft where I couldn't even tell the vessel was moving.

I dozed, waking periodically and hearing nothing. Excitement burst inside me. Maybe there were no people on board! Sitting with my head tipped back, I listened. No voices. No one passing by the closet. The ship must be operated by droids. I'd give it a little longer, then I'd locate the captain's stateroom and break into the safe.

Sleeping, I dreamed of returning home and buying the cure for Mom. She wouldn't be sick anymore. I wouldn't lose her.

I woke sometime later in utter silence.

When I deemed I'd remained hidden long enough, I crept from the closet and continued down the hall, cautiously opening each door I passed, but not finding anything that looked like a main stateroom. This was a big ship, however, so it might not be located on this level. Only the low hum of the engines and the shallow slap of my shoes on the floor broke the silence.

I was hugging the wall, approaching an intersection, when a bang rang out ahead. Shrinking into my skin, I wrangled with my spit, too afraid to swallow in case it was overheard.

The sound wasn't repeated, telling me it could be nothing. Space debris hitting the outer hull. A droid smacking against a wall.

With my nerve endings twitching, I pulled my knife,

the weight of it giving me the boost of courage I needed to continue forward.

Muffled voices echoed from a location I couldn't define, someone telling another person they were going to the galley.

Shit. There were people—*aliens*—on the ship!

Determined to hide, I flew to the intersection and raced around the corner.

I smacked into something big and warm and full of snarls. Huge bronze hands groped for my arms.

A shriek burst from me, and I flailed, reeling backward. I stared up at a freakin' ogre.

I only caught glimpses of burnished copper skin, an eye patch, and silver hair as he swept out his booted foot, nearly taking my legs out from underneath me.

With a guttural cry, I hitched my knife forward. It sunk into flesh, and the fuming alien ogre groaned. Dralian species, if I wasn't mistaken. They'd gotten caught up in the human-Evarian war and their people were nearly wiped out. It looked like I was doing my best to eliminate another.

And man, was this Dralian male pissed. He sputtered and fumed, glaring at me while clutching my forearm.

A blue and white fluffy creature sat on his right shoulder, watching me with sapphire blue eyes. It hissed in my direction, but who could blame it?

While I guppy breathed, the muscular alien yanked aside a corner of his sleeveless leather vest, revealing rows of rippling muscles. Man, what pecs! Leave it to me to notice at a time like this.

Blood seeped around my blade still embedded in the right side of his belly. Such a shame to ruin his washboard perfection.

He wrenched out the knife and tucked it into the waistband of his low-slung pants.

His glare from his unpatched eye pinned me in place.

"Sorry?" I whimpered, wiggling to break free from his grip. "I didn't mean to poke you."

He jerked me against his taut frame. With a simple flex, he tossed me onto his left shoulder. The fluffy cat-like creature leaned around the alien's head, its whiskers twitching. It released a long series of howls until the alien stroked the creature's spine.

Pivoting, the Dralian ogre strode down the hall, leaving a trail of amber blood droplets on the plexi floor.

"You, human youngling," he snarled. "Are about to get your ass smacked."

Get your copy NOW!